STEPHEN MENENDEZ

Journey Into Darkness
A Tunnel Rat's Story

St. John's Press

Copyright© 2004 by Stephen Menendez

ALL RIGHTS RESERVED — No part of this book may be reproduced or transmitted in any form or by any means, electronic or mechanical, including photocopying, recording, or by any information storage and retrieval system, without the written permission of the author.

Edited and Published by
St. John's Press
5318 Tori Park Dr.
Cottondale, AL 35453
Tel: 205-507-4633 E-Mail: Sjpress@aol.com
www.stjohnspress.com

Cover photograph, Stephen Menendez
Cover design by St. John's Press
Edited by Charles J. Boyle

Printed in the USA
Journey Into Darkness, A Tunnel Rat's Story/Menendez, Stephen
St. John's Press

1. United States-Fiction- History-Vietnam War-Tunnels-Autobiography

First Edition – 2004

The names contained in this story are fictional. Any similarities to real persons either living or deceased are purely coincidental and not intended to represent any living characters.

ISBN 0-9710551-6-5

In Gratitude

My everlasting gratitude to my wife Linda for the many hours she spent typing my story and encouraging me to tell it. I would not have written this without the constant support of Jim Seegraves. I must also thank the men with whom I served in the 3rd Platoon of Charlie Company, 3rd Battalion, 22nd Infantry, 25th Infantry Division. They are the greatest men I've ever known.

Contents

	Dedication	v
	Contents	vii
	Preface	ix
I	Looking Back	1
II	Wire Guard	10
III	Ambush	15
IV	First Tunnel	23
V	Counter Attack	36
VI	Assembly	47
VII	The Party Begins	58
VIII	The VC General	70
IX	Our Former Enemy	77
X	Special Invitation	93
XI	Return to Vietnam	97
XII	The Making of a Tunnel Rat	101
XIII	Tunnel Rat Exam	114
XIV	A Really Good Show	120
XV	Vietnam Dinner Party	126
XVI	Payback	151
	Epilogue	158

Preface

I often reconstruct the events of Vietnam in my memory; it seems like only yesterday. I think of the guys I served with, all of whom I remember as wonderful friends. They were from all areas of the United States. Most of them were fresh from high school or undecided about their future. They hadn't moved quick enough to enroll in college and become draft deferred—nor did they act cowardly—hiding out somewhere. We became brothers forever because of Vietnam.

Now, almost 30 years later, we are going to reunite for a reunion; an assembly of men that will surely stir memories and emotions. Nevertheless, we are anxious to meet each other again, but in a much more comfortable setting than the jungles of Vietnam.

These men, who once felt themselves invincible and fought the good fight, may now show feelings long masked by events, careers, and family. Still, they will come to the reunion. They must. Only another Vietnam veteran can fully understand and appreciate them.

Anyone who reads this story should recognize the value of these men ... these heroes. I was a witness to the trials of the men of Charlie Company, and their valor on the battlefield is unquestionable. Yes, we complained. We didn't want to be there, but we stuck together as brothers and we did our job.

If you should ever meet one of these men, he may not look like a hero. He is commonplace among the crowd; he has taken his place in society and time has its way with soldiers. Nevertheless, when you shake his hand, just say, "Welcome home." It says it all.

I

LOOKING BACK

The phone rang twice before I answered. A man's voice, unfamiliar, but a little anxious, asked if I might be Mr. 'Shorty' Mendez who served with Charlie Company in Vietnam, "around '69 or '70."

A little bewildered but curious, I thought for a moment before I responded. This might be the call I had waited for but thought would never come. So many years had passed since Vietnam, and I had never heard from any of the guys. Early on, the few VFW and American Legion halls I wandered into were useless attempts at trying to find another Vietnam veteran; maybe somebody I had served with. It seemed that only WWII and Korean vets "belonged" back in the 1970s. Nice guys, but I yearned to meet with other men who had served in Vietnam. Learning firsthand about the "greatest generation" and how they whipped the Nazi's, wasn't what I was looking for. Eventually, I quit looking. I had kept my caller waiting too long.

"I believe I am," I said. "Friends call me by that nickname. Who are you ... why do you ask?"

"Shorty... this is Stuart, Stuart Simmons. Remember? I'm looking for fellow soldiers who served with me in Charlie Company. I'm on a committee and we're planning a reunion.... Hope it's you."

Stuart Simmons. Sure.... I had forgotten the name but not the man. The sound of his voice stirred instant flashes of jungles and tunnels; rain and heat, and men with rifles in their hands. Stuart was from Iowa, I remembered.

"Hello Stuart. Sure I remember. How are you? What kind of reunion? Where, when?"

"Well, glad you still know me. Shoot, making these calls isn't the easiest thing to do, but I'm helping to find our guys, get them together for a gathering of sorts. You were easy to find ... not like some guys ... hiding out and all."

The earlier tension had passed. I was excited and so was Stuart. We were now chattering like a couple of machine guns firing alternating bursts of bullets.

"I've thought a lot about you, Shorty. I hope the years have been kind. What are you doing these days? I'm an accountant ... used my GI Bill."

"Life is good, Stuart. I'm in law enforcement."

"You mean you're a cop? It figures."

"Yeah, I've got to have a 'pistola' and a big flashlight in my hand, remember?"

We laughed. It was so good to hear Stuart's voice. We had shared a lot in Vietnam. Stuart was a country boy from Middle America. He was strong, wholesome and likable; the way they grow them out in Iowa. I could see his fresh face, his nervous hands moving through his sandy hair as we sat on ambush or rummaged through enemy base camps. In addition, I could see him incessantly chewing on those tropical grasses. "Hayseed," we called him.

"Remember you, Stuart? How could I ever forget?"

"Say, Shorty, do you remember Sergeant Browning? Lowell Browning? He was from Tennessee, I think. We called him 'Rocky Top.' And how about that city slicker, Standish? Gary was it? ...out of New York, maybe. I'm looking all over the country for these guys. I've been getting some help from a guy out in Portland. Say, you and Standish were pretty 'tight' over there. Have you ever heard from him?"

Had I heard from him? No, but Gary was the object of my search when I visited those veteran clubs. Tight was not the word; it could hardly describe it.

"No, never heard a thing, Stuart. Wish I had, we were good friends. We got there the same day. New York might have swallowed him up after 'Nam. He was too cool ... too nice for those mean streets. I wonder if he ever got his braces? He used to complain that the army wouldn't fix his teeth. ...said he was handicapped and ought to be sent home. Heck, he almost convinced Sergeant Browning."

"Oh yeah.... He took the same teeth home that he came with. Everybody had some reason to go home. Sarge didn't buy any of it."

Overwhelmed by hearing Stuart's voice and such familiar names, my mind went completely blank for a few moments.

"Hello, brother, are you still there?" Stuart asked.

"Yes, I just got such a rush of memories that I lost my thoughts for a sec."

Sure, it's just that Standish ... Sergeant Browning.... Guys like that never leave your mind. I remember them all. Sergeant Browning was my platoon sergeant when I first arrived in Vietnam. What a guy..."

"Hang on Stuart, I'm having a moment," I said. It was all coming so fast, I needed to compose myself. I took the portable phone and moved a few steps to my den. Flopping down in my favorite easy chair, I looked around to see if my wife would notice my few tears, my weakening knees. I could hide very little from Linda, but she didn't know about the quiet longing I held for my buddies. No one did.

"I understand, little buddy. I've had my moments too," Stuart said.

You can't stop a mind when it's been kick-started. My thoughts spiraled downward, backward, and into scenes I thought I had buried. I was going back to Vietnam, powerless to stop it and maybe not wanting to.

Journey Into Darkness

Charlie Company was occupying a small patrol base next to the Cambodian border when I arrived. The chopper ride was exciting, but became downright scary as we approached our landing spot. The pilot drove his machine at high speed, just clearing the treetops as he banked and rolled left and right. There were six of us on board, all fresh from the States. Everyone seemed to be calm, as if they knew what it was all about. I held on for dear life. Maybe he just felt my fear, but one of the door gunners turned to me, smiled and gave me a thumbs-up sign. I felt better after that and the landing was uneventful.

Following their lead, I stooped over like the other guys and raced away from the windy blasts of the helicopter blades. Without my rucksack, my rifle, and all of the gear I carried, it felt like the blades would have sucked me right up into them. Out of breath, I arrived in the middle of the company command post along with the others.

"Where we at?" a tall guy asked.

Wondering much the same thing, I expected someone would greet us and explain things very quickly. It was getting late in the afternoon and I wanted to be settled in before dark. In a few minutes, a tall, slim fellow approached and his stride suggested he had important business on his mind.

"All right, boys.... Welcome to Vietnam," he said. He smiled at all of us, but did not ask our names or extend his hand. The smile faded and he began his lecture: "Boys, I'm Sergeant Browning, your Platoon Sergeant. The Lieutenant will be along soon and he'll talk to you, too. For right now, I'll tell you a few things that might keep you alive. ...get you back home again some day. Pay attention. You are at Fire Support Base Crooks, situated up against the Cambodian Border."

Using his M-16 rifle as a pointer, he gestured toward the jungle wall and continued. "See, it's right that way, about two clicks. (kilometers) It's a nasty jungle out there. We protect the artillery here, run patrols all day looking for 'Victor Charlie.'

Looking Back

We run ambushes all night, trying to kill him before he kills us ... and a dozen other uncivilized things. The Viet Cong and North Vietnamese Regulars use that jungle to infiltrate into South Vietnam. Our job is to catch them ... blow 'em away. You don't do that, he'll do it to you. Any questions so far?"

I had a million of them, but I decided to let someone else ask. Army sergeants had a way of making you feel foolish when you asked a stupid question. Most questions were "stupid" I had learned in basic training.

The thin man stepped forward, put something in his mouth and chewed it slowly, savoring the taste. I noticed his broad shoulders and thought it rather odd that he could be so wide at the top and narrow around the waist. I hadn't paid much attention to him on the chopper.

"Yeah, Sarge, can I ask where the hell we are? I'm expecting a package from home. Do we get mail out here?" he said.

"Fair question," Sergeant Browning said. "You're in Charlie Company, 3rd Battalion 22nd Infantry. They call us 'Chargin' Charlie' and you'll soon learn why. You're also part of the 25th Infantry Division if you didn't know that. Yes, you'll get mail from time to time, but the best thing to do is not to think about home too much. It's depressing. Keep you mind on your business.

"Cool.... Okay," the thin man said.

Sergeant Browning continued: "Now.... you are in an area of operations called War Zone C. We're 'bout in the middle of it. If you came to shoot communists, you'll get a fill of it 'fore long."

Somewhere in "War Zone C, I mused. Well, that would impress my mother. Names like that didn't mean much to a rookie like me back in 1969. The war had been going on for a long time and most guys my age had never imagined they'd be looking at such emerald green tropical forests—forests that would become our home for the next twelve months.

We had read about Vietnam and knew terms like "Ho Chi Minh Trail," "Cambodian Border," and "Tet," from television newscasts. We had even studied a little bit about it in high school. Now I was looking dead at that war. Reality was sinking in and it enveloped me completely that afternoon. I shed my innocence right there, staring at that formidable but beautiful landscape. *I'm going to make it*, I decided.

Sergeant Lowell Browning was young, maybe 23 years old. Nevertheless, he was obviously in charge, despite his youth. His voice, mannerisms and his southern dialect suggested he was as human like the rest of us; he just had the stripes. I decided that he knew what he was talking about and I'd better pay attention to him.

"Be firm but fair," was something I had learned in a leadership class back in advanced infantry training. Sergeant Browning appeared to fit that ideal. In fact, shortly after the meeting broke up and we were assigned to our squads, he gave me "wire guard" for my first night at the camp. I understood it to be an honor or a special privilege of some kind to have wire guard, especially if you just got there. I assumed it meant I stood out from the crowd.

Later that evening I sensed the exhaustion from my travel, and especially from the digging I'd been doing. We were in three-man positions and shared the work of improving our foxhole. The moist brown earth made for easy digging, but it wasn't very interesting employment. It was, however, necessary and I knew it. After a while, I remarked that we had a hole as big as a house. "We need to buy some furniture," I said.

No one laughed. Someone said "Yeah," but that was all. I guess Sarge was right; the place could be depressing. I didn't know anyone, and no one had talked to me about anything substantial. Still in doubt about my special mission for later that evening, I decided to ask the guys who had been in the squad for a while if it was good to have wire guard. I didn't ask what it was, as I didn't want to show them how little I knew.

Looking Back

They said any "green weenie" would consider it an honor or a promotion if they got wire guard on their first night.

"You should consider yourself lucky," someone said. So, I did. I concluded that it was duty watching some wire or radio equipment. Maybe I could finish reading that novel I had started on the plane. Still wondering, I settled down in my sandbagged bunker for a few minutes nap. Sergeant Browning said he'd brief me before I went out. I sat upright: *Out! Out where!* I didn't see anything but a wall of green stuff beyond our defensive "berm" line and it was getting as dark as a Florida swamp. The night came on fast in Vietnam.

"Sorry, Private Mendez," Sergeant Browning said as he kicked my boot. "You'll be leaving our defensive perimeter in a few minutes. You'll spend the night as a listening post, just beyond our barbed wire. You'll be our eyes and ears..." He grinned again.

"That's wire guard?"

"Don't sweat it. I know the guys told you it was a cinch ... something special. And, it is. We need to keep 'Charlie' off our back and listening posts are just one of the ways to do it. We have patrols out, too."

I swallowed hard. *Just me? Alone all night?*

"Without being disrespectful, Sergeant, may I ask why you picked me? I just got here. I don't even know which way is north, south, or anything else. I might get lost." Visions of me walking into the woods and never returning flashed through my mind. I could see tigers and giant snakes eating me up.

"You'll have some help," Mendez. See... trouble is... all of our guys are bushed from patrolling, ambushes and guard duty every day and every night. You new guys come along and we are damn happy to have the fresh blood. Nothing personal. Get a little rest, I'll get you when it's time to go."

It seemed like only minutes had passed when someone was pulling on one of my boots. I looked up and saw one of the new guys I met on my chopper ride. It was thin man with the broad shoulders.

"I'm Gary Standish," he said as I shook his extended hand. "I call New York home ... 5th and Broadway ... ever been there?"

I stood up and brushed off the dirt. "No, can't say I have. I never thought I'd leave my Wisconsin estate. Are you my wire guard helper?"

"Yeah, man, that's me. It'll be cool. The guys have been telling me all we need to know. It's a 'sugar cookie' they say."

I felt good having someone to talk too, but I realized my wire guard partner didn't know any more about it than I did. He said he remembered me from the flight, and, like me, I was the only man he felt he knew at the moment. I stood upright when he said Sergeant Browning told him to find, "Super Short." "You must be him," he said. "You're the only one under five feet tall around this camp."

I told him I had to suffer through "short" name jokes all my life. I had heard so many remarks about my height, or lack of it, that it ceased to be an issue long ago.

"I really don't mind you calling me short," I said, "unless you want to get snotty about it. Call me any short name you want, just say it with a smile. I've been calling you the "Thin Man."

Gary Standish laughed and we were at ease with one another. He admitted that he didn't know anything about the mission and would have preferred to stay at home this night. His sense of humor was good and I liked his attitude. "What did the sergeant tell you about this wire guard? Where are we going? What do we do?" he asked.

"Oh, it's just some kind of radio duty or something. A real 'sham' detail, I hear. It's sort of like burning crap." I smiled inwardly. *Call me 'Super Short,' will he?*

"Burn crap?" Standish asked. "What's that about?"

"I haven't done it yet, but you are aware, aren't you, that in Vietnam, human waste is not flushed down a toilet. My older brother's a Vietnam vet. He told me about it."

I explained that the water table was too high to build latrines the old fashioned way. Instead, outhouses were built that held metal drums to catch the refuse. Each day, a soldier pulled out the drums, doused the contents with diesel fuel and set it on fire. As it smoldered, the soldier stirred the contents with a stick to keep it aflame. The foul odor clogged his nostrils, seeped into his clothing and spread across the entire camp. In spite of it being a nasty duty, it was a good trade-off from being in the field, on patrol, or being shot at. Most soldiers didn't complain when they were assigned to the crap burning detail. They pinched their nose and gave thanks to the Almighty.

"I've wondered where we shit," Standish said.

I admitted to him that since I wasn't up on all of the G.I. lingo, I could only assume that we'd have an easy detail that night. I really didn't know. We began gathering our equipment for the guard detail. I made sure to put some extra goodies in my pack for a late snack. I had a flashlight, so I took my book. Maybe I'd do some reading.

Standish said he still had some oatmeal cookies his mother had sent. "The mail is in," he said. "Want some?"
He handed me a couple handfuls of cookie crumbs. "Seems the postal system was a little rough on these."

We stopped laughing when Sergeant Browning entered our bunker. "It's time to brief you two on your duties. Ready?"

"Yes, Sir."

II

WIRE GUARD

We listened as Sergeant Browning described wire guard duty. We looked at each other, wondering if each other's hair was standing up on the back of our necks. He wasn't exaggerating when he said it was no laughing matter. "As soon as it's dark, you two will climb over the berm," he said. "... the dirt mounds that surround our camp. Crawl down that narrow ditch. It runs maybe fifty feet out to the first strand of concertina wire. Be careful, there's about four rows of razor wire."

"How do we get through it?" I asked.

"Best you can, Mendez. You shouldn't have a problem with that. Crawl under it. Hell, a man like you can probably walk under it standing up."

I should have been insulted, but somehow Sergeant Browning's remark didn't offend me. He said it almost as if it were a compliment.

A man like me....

"At the end of the ditch is a foxhole," he continued, after checking my reaction. "You gotta find it. It's maybe five feet in diameter and three feet deep. Check it for snakes or anything before ya'all get in it. Your job is to stay alert and let us know by radio if anything's moving ... any VC comin' our way." He spit brown tobacco juice and shifted his rifle to his hip, muzzle in the air.

Silence!

I imagined Standish and me sitting in a foxhole all night, ten-thousand miles away from home, in a strange land full of snakes, bugs, and bullets. I could feel the sweat beginning to fill my armpits and run down my lower back. I wondered if Standish felt the same.

"Well... Any questions?" Sergeant Browning asked.

"Yes, Sergeant," I said. "What if we hear something or see something out there?"

"Well.... Just be damn sure you do hear or see something. No false alarms, OK? Call on the radio and alert us if you're real sure. Then crawl like hell back to the berm. Remember to let the guys on the line know you're coming in so they don't shoot you. That's happened before."

"Oh, Great. You mean our own guys might shoot us?" Standish said. "We have enemy out to our front, and trigger happy guys at our back. What else do we have to worry about?"

"Snakes," I said.

Sergeant Browning assured us we'd do just fine and left us sweating. Darkness came all too soon. We knew we had to go, so with a shrug of the shoulders and a prayer on our lips, over the berm we went. We could hear the other guys whispering, saying things such as, "Watch out for 'bunker dogs'" or "don't call us, we'll call you." A guy they called Roser said, "If you don't come back, can I have your breakfast ... your smokes?"

I'm sure they knew how we were feeling, as they must have felt the same way on their first guard duty in the jungles of Vietnam. Having fun with the new guys was their way of relieving their own anxiety.

An eerie blackness covered the base camp. Night had fallen and all was quiet. The men had settled down and the silence was broken only by occasional animal sounds coming out of those thick, black woods. I had never heard such strange noises: Exotic birds screeched, tree lizards barked out odd messages and bugs hummed everywhere. It only added to my anxiety. Standish and I looked at each other, swallowed hard, and began moving down the ditch.

In spite of the dark, the going was not too bad. Many soldiers before us had beaten a path to the position. We didn't crawl and we didn't walk. Hunched over, we shuffled forward five steps, then sideways two steps, and then turned around for a bit. I felt like a thousand eyes were upon me. *They're everywhere!*

I tripped and fell. Something wrapped around my leg and wouldn't let go. It was alive and had its mind set on capturing and swallowing me. I was certain it was a giant snake. I reached down to fight it off, only to discover that a length of barbed wire had wrapped around my leg.

"Jesus Madre!"

"Be quiet," Standish admonished me as I shrieked. Helping to remove the wire from my leg, he pulled me up and commented: "Our guys will think we're VC and the VC will think we're Poncho Villa. No more cookies for you."

We were soon sitting in the foxhole, our eyes the size of saucers. We must have sat staring out through the darkness for an hour before either of us whispered a word.

"My mother was right," Standish said.

"Why's that?" I asked.

"Mush for brains. I should have gone to college ... Canada."

"Yeah, my mother said I should always wear clean underwear in case I went to the hospital. Right now, I don't know if I can live up to that. It's spooky as hell out here."

We fell into silence for a few moments, thinking about our situation. Finally, Standish spoke up. "I'm getting out of here as soon as I can, you'll see."

"I'll go with you. How are you going to do that?"

"I need braces on my teeth, didn't you notice? They'll have to send me to the dentist."

"Standish! We're in the middle of nowhere. Where are you going to find an orthodontist?"

"Broadway and 50th, I know a good one. The army literature said free medical and dental care. I'll sue if they don't send me to my dentist."

The levity and small talk helped ease our fears and we shared information about ourselves, our families, and our expectations for the future. We became lifelong friends through the process, without knowing it at the time.

We decided on two-hour shifts and I would stay awake while Standish tried to sleep. He lay back against the wall of the foxhole to get as comfortable as possible. Before long, I could hear his heavy breathing. He was sound asleep, and that came as no surprise. We were drained from the heat, not to mention the nervous energy we had used up. I passed the two hours listening to every bug and creature that crawled within fifty feet of me. My mind raced.

I know they are just on the other side of that wire watching me. The Japanese were masters of night vision during World War II. These guys are too, I'm sure. ...stands to reason ... wish I could see them. Maybe I should wake Standish....

My wristwatch said my two hours were up. I poked Standish with a stick and he awoke with a jerk.

"What the hey...!"

"Your turn," I said. "Nothing happening out here ... all quiet on the jungle front." I yawned and settled into the same position Standish had been in. It was slightly warm from his body heat and I noticed for the first time how cool it was at night. It was such a contrast from the scorching heat of the day. I closed my eyes and got comfortable. I slept for only a few minutes when I was startled by a strange noise; a very light continuous crunching sound. I listened with great intent, sure that someone or something was crunching the dried grass outside the wire. Rubbing my eyes, I slowly opened them against my will. All I could see was black. There was no moon to provide any shadows or to see movement.

I whispered, "Standish, are you awake?"

"Of course," he said.

"Well, what's that crunching I've been hearing?"

"Don't know.... I haven't heard anything ... you dreaming?"

My nerves were playing tricks, so I settled back to try to sleep.

"Crunch. Crunch." There it was again.

"Standish," I said.

"Yeah."

"Don't you hear that sound?"

"Don't hear nothing."

"I know I heard something ... should we call it in?" Too nervous to sleep, I decided I would pull watch with Standish. Sleep just didn't seem to be in the plan for this night. I forgot about reading my book, too. Sure enough, moments later I heard the same sound. I sat up and peered into the darkness, trying to locate the source of the noise. The more I listened the more I realized the sound came from Gary's exact position.

"Hey, Standish..."

"Yeah, what ya want?"

"Are you doing something ... making those noises?"

"Naw, I ain't doing anything."

I moved up next to him and sure enough, the noise was coming from him. "Are you eating something, Standish?"

"Just some stale cookie crumbs."

"Well, chew quietly. I'm sure if I can hear you chew, the VC can."

"OK. I'll write home and ask my mom to send some of those soft gooey cookies."

Standish and I figured we were both too nervous to sleep anymore and stayed on watch together. Through quiet conversation, we learned each other's inner thoughts and discussed how we felt about the war. We talked about school, we talked about the girls we knew, and we talked about sports. In fact, we talked about anything that came to mind. I began to call him Gary and when he called me Shorty, I felt good. I had a friend at last. From that night on and for the rest of the year, we seldom left each other's side.

The sun came up and we returned to the safety of the encampment. I saw the guy named Roser standing near the bunker just as we came over the berm. Now toughened and confident by the wire guard experience, I shouted: "Hey, Roser, guess I'll eat my chow myself this morning. But, if you're hungry, I have some real good cookies that Gary's Mom sent him."

III

AMBUSH

Stuart Simmons' voice crackled across the phone. He understood my flashbacks and snapped me back into reality from time to time. I uttered an occasional, "Yeah or "Uh huh," then suddenly recognized the name, Eric Schmitter.

"Schmitter.... Lieutenant Schmitter," Stuart repeated. He was from California. You remember.... Our Lieutenant with the freckles. We just called him 'L.T.'"

"Oh, yeah, how could I forget, L.T.?" I said. "He was a good man, a first-class leader ... never forget him."

Lieutenant Schmitter seemed like such a distant person when I first met him, but soldiers at war usually keep a little distance between each other. It hurts real bad when a friend is killed. There is less heartache that way.

Lieutenant Schmitter was simply called by the letters L.T. In the Infantry, we close the social gap between the platoon leader and the men by simply calling them, L.T. It's actually a gesture of respect, bestowed upon the leader by his subordinates. It's a way of saying, "We know you're the boss, but we also know you are human and just like us. We can blame you if things go wrong, and praise you when they go smoothly."

The task of an Infantry Platoon Leader in combat is a dangerous and difficult occupation. It takes intelligence, toughness and courage. It takes a patriotic fervor, mental and physical endurance, and a genuine concern for the welfare of men. Lieutenant Schmitter lived up to all of this and more.

Not long after I had arrived, L.T. came to our bunker and said he had volunteered our platoon for a night ambush.

Volunteered! I thought he was nuts.

Sergeant Browning asked, "Why? We've just finished a three-day patrol. This will be our first good night's sleep."

"Outside please, Sergeant Browning," L.T. said. "We need to talk."

We could tell from the tone of his voice that L.T. was winning the war of words. Sergeant Browning came back into the bunker and said, "It's 1500 hours now; get ready to crack some eggs. We move out at 1630 sharp."

We just glared. You didn't second-guess Sergeant Browning and we only called him "Sarge" when he wasn't within earshot. I presumed 'cracking eggs' was his way of saying we might see some action. That afternoon we gathered near the perimeter for a final briefing. Sarge arrived just ahead of the platoon leader and spoke quickly. He sensed we needed to hear something.

"From what I hear, this one ought to be a little hairy. I know you're tired, but stay alert. Don't go getting lazy on me. You guys are the best platoon in the company—more experienced. That's why we got picked."

I figured it was all talk, just to justify this surprise duty.

"Experienced? Who? Us?" Gary said. "He sure hasn't looked at me lately."

"Well, we're kind of experienced," I said. "True, we just picked up two new guys, but then there is Roser and the other guys. They've been here for at least a month longer than us."

I looked around at my squad members: The men who might live or die alongside of me. No matter how new you were to Vietnam, it didn't take long to become a veteran—an "old timer." A month in Vietnam was a lifetime. A boy became a man very fast.

We all understood that the only way to survive was to hang together. We did have six men with experience, so I didn't worry too much. We had a medic, a radioman, and a couple of guys I didn't know very well. But in Vietnam, you didn't have to know each other well; you took care of a guy if he was down, whether you knew him or not. When I told Gary about the new guys, he said that they were on their second tour of duty in Vietnam.

"Great, let's stick close to those two."

Sarge ordered the platoon on its way. We "humped" out the camp's main gate and headed west. We moved slowly, avoiding the trails, cutting the thick foliage with machetes, and using men out on the flanks to keep the bad guys off of us if they were laying in wait. Nothing happened and in about an hour we reached a small clearing. Sarge must have been reading my mind: I needed a break. I was relieved to be free of the underbrush and was catching my breath when he said, "Pull in here and set up for the night."

We all looked at each other; it seemed like such an unusually short trip. We were, however, very happy to follow his orders. Even a one-hour walk with the load we carried was tiresome.

"Hump" and "Grunt" are two words that came out of Vietnam. If you looked at us, with the equipment we carried in our rucksacks, you'd think we were all hunchbacks. That sack made a huge mound on our backs and the word "hump" evolved naturally. It was an accurate description, too. I carried about 85-pounds of ammunition and equipment; some men carried more. In addition to claymore mines, grenades, and clips of ammunition, we all carried a belt or two of M-60 machine gun ammo.

I sucked up water like a sponge in that environment and carried four canteens of water around my waist. My gas mask bounced against my leg as I walked, but Sarge insisted we carry them at all times. In my pack, I had stuffed a nylon poncho liner to wrap around me on cool nights. I had been given a lightweight nylon hammock from one of the guys going home. From time to time, I was able to string it between two trees. It was a wonderful invention; I slept like a log in that thing. My rain poncho was handy for making shade over a position, but it was useless during the heavy monsoon rains. Draped over us, it became as wet on the inside as it did on the outside. But we carried them, nevertheless. They were useful for carrying wounded and wrapping dead men in.

Mostly I carried ammunition in that pack. A three-day supply of bullets and nine boxes of C-rations just about filled me out. There were also the old letters from home, writing paper, a toothbrush, razor and the ever-present cookie crumbs from Gary's mother lode. I must have been carrying as much as my own body weight sometimes, but I felt lucky; some guys had to carry a radio or heavy mortar tubes and base plates in addition to their load.

Grunt? That was the sound we made when we stood up under the bulky load. The word became a title ... a badge of honor. I was proud to be a Grunt.

Looking for the best ambush site, we moved a little farther, walking along the edge of a tree line. We finally stopped at the edge of some bushy woods. It must have looked good to the leaders.

"This is it," Sarge said. "Set up an 'L'"

Tactically, an L-shaped ambush was considered to be ideal. The enemy, if they were unlucky enough to walk into the trap, were caught from the front and the flank at the same time. Tactical considerations aside, everyone looked for the best position for themselves. They not only wanted a good spot to fire from; they wanted to be comfortable. There might even be a chance to catch some sleep.

Finding a spot along the leg of the L, I dropped my pack and took off my heavy helmet. Phil Murphy, a giant of a man from Alabama, carried a pallet of 90-millimeter high explosive rounds and the cannon to go with it. He clomped up to me.

"That's my spot, Shorty. I need it for the cannon, ya'all got to go someplace else."

I didn't argue. The 90-millimeter took priority in positions and he just seemed too frightening to argue with. I moved about twenty feet to my left. The earth looked comfortable and it had a small depression in which I could lay low.

"Hey, Shorty, that's my spot," Dave Garrison announced. "I picked it before we got here, any questions?" Dave was Murphy's assistant. I moved again.

Every place I picked to set up, one of the more experienced guys said they had already picked that spot and FNG's (Freaking New Guys) had to set up at the end of the ambush line. The "end-o-the-line" was not the best place to be if there was any action. You were kind of hanging out there with nobody by your side. I moved my rucksack to the outer edge of the line where I found Gary. He had a big smile on his face and pointing to a nice grassy spot next to him. "Guess we should just stick with each other," Gary said. "Care for an oatmeal cookie? "Mom just sent them."

I took one, shoved it in my mouth, and flopped down; glad to be next to Gary Standish. We prepared a shallow foxhole and cut brush so that we could see from a prone position. I placed my claymore mine about 20 feet to my front and ran the detonator wire back to our position. Gary covered me while I worked out in front. I covered him while he placed his mine.

We did everything by the book, pleasing Sergeant Browning and L.T. when they came by to check our position. "Good work, men," Sarge said. "I wish everyone was as hard 'a workers as you two city boys."I was pleased with myself and mentioned to Gary that I actually hoped to see some action that night. So far, I had only heard a few explosions in the distance, watch artillery flares illuminate the jungle canopy at night, and helped evacuate a guy who had accidentally poked himself in the eye with the front sight of his M-16 rifle. The war hadn't begun for me. Gary and I made small talk until the sun set over Cambodia.

Suddenly it was so still, you could hear the men next to us breathing. Then I heard water splashing. I poked Gary in the ribs.

"You awake?

"Almost."

"What's that sound?"

"What sound?"

"Like water..."

"That's just Murphy taking a piss. He drinks a case of beer every day."

"Beer? Where's he get beer out here?"

"He carries it in his ruck. In the morning he'll be by to hold you up for your C-rations 'cause all he carries is ammo and beer."

"Really!"

"Yeah, he stays buzzed. Now be quiet and let me sleep. You're watching, right?"

"Oh, yeah."

I thought about Murphy and how a cold beer would go good right then. I thought about home and football and church and God, and I wondered why I hadn't listened to my mother and become a priest. Then I heard it!

"Mark! Mark!" the odd cry screeched from out of the jungle night. It was within 15 feet of me and shattered our protective silence as well as my nerves.

"Gary, what the heck was that...! You hear that?"

Gary was sitting upright, fumbling for the detonator to his claymore. "VC, I think. They're calling out ... trying to see if anyone answers..."

"Mark! Mark!" The cry came again.

"Maybe we ought to blow our mines," Gary said. "They're right on top of us."

"Not yet, the others hear it too. Wait on them," I said.

"Mark! Mark!"

"Shut the hell up," Murphy yelled out from his position

"Fuck you," came the instant reply from the jungle. Then, "Mark! Mark!"

"This is weird, Shorty. ...Crazy," Gary said.

Sweat rolled down my face and dripped from my nose.

I agreed with Gary. We should blow our mines, fire a magazine in the direction of the enemy, and then run like hell.

Someone touched me on my shoulder and I froze. I was dead and I knew it. They had sneaked up from behind. *Yikes!*

"Take it easy, Mendez. You too, Standish. That's just a tree lizard." It was Sergeant Browning, making his rounds and settling the men. I was so glad to see him I wanted to hug him. How he managed to sneak up on us like that kept me thinking for days afterward.

"I figured you new guys might get the heebe jeebes from that "fuck you" lizard."

"What did you call it?" I asked.

"Well.... It's a tree lizard ... like an Iguana kinda thing. Big sucker.... They are good eatin', the Vietnamese say. That's him calling for his momma ... maybe his mate. It sounds like it's saying 'Fuck you' so the guys give it that name. The noise comes from down in its throat. I figured it might shake you so I just dropped by. You didn't know about it?"

Standish didn't waste a second: "Yeah, I know about them. We have them in upstate New York, too. ...didn't bother me."

I couldn't see him, but I knew Sergeant Browning was grinning.

"OK, men," he said. "Then be careful of the thing if it gets on the ground. I hear over in Alpha Company they lost a man to one of them lizards ... found his body with no legs the next morning. Ripped him all to hell, they say. Stay awake, I'll be checking on you later." Sergeant Browning crawled backward away from our position.

Gary and I drew closer. "Was he kidding or what, Shorty? Do you think that thing really eats you?"

"I don't know. What do they do to people in New York?"

As it turned out, the ambush was a quiet one. I Guess the VC had no desire to pass our way that night. The only activity was the occasional call of the lizard, which remained high up in the tree, and Murphy relieving himself every hour on the hour. Gary and I stayed wide-awake all night.

Tired, dirty, and still a little perturbed with the extra ambush detail, we reentered our base camp around noon that day. We were cleaning rifles and equipment and doing some typical complaining about the ambush when we noticed Sergeant Browning and L.T. coming our way. We expected more bad news. You could cut through the tension with a bayonet.

"Platoon meeting in ten minutes. Go collect the other men," Sergeant Browning said.

Assembled around our fighting bunkers, the men were making bets whether we were going on another ambush or if L.T. had volunteered us for something else. Lieutenant Schmitter studied his notebook for a moment, and then finally spoke: "OK men, our mission for the next three days... " He paused, looked up and directly into each face. Apparently, he sensed our mood.

"Our mission," L.T. continued, "is to secure the base camp while the other platoons work a three-day ambush. You're off the hook. ...caught a break for once."

Stunned, we didn't grasp the meaning of his words for a few seconds, or the significance of our new mission. Suddenly, in chorus, we realized it meant we weren't going back out into the jungle. We could sleep all day with minimal time on guard duty.

A cheer went up and we began slapping each other on the back. "High-fives" were everywhere. It was "sham" time. Later, while we were all sharing stories, jokes and a few cold beers, Sarge let us know that it was our Lieutenant who pulled off this little vacation. He knew that by volunteering us for the ambush the night before, we would be skipped over for the next mission.

It was a deal he had worked out with Captain Stells, our Company Commander. He was looking out for us and I never doubted him again. Gary and I agreed that our L.T. was a pretty decent guy after all. We all began to understand a little more of what makes some leaders good and others not so good. Sometimes it's hard to see, but after that episode, we all had great respect for our L.T.

IV

FIRST TUNNEL

*O*ur **little holiday ended much too quick. It seemed as** though the three days merged into one as we had little to do except eat, sleep, write letters home and pull a little guard duty. On the afternoon of the third day, we received an urgent radio call that one of our platoons was in trouble.

"First Platoon's in deep ... firefight west of here!" Sergeant Browning yelled as he raced between our positions. "Get your gear!"

Without question, we quickly gathered our ammunition and equipment. In ten minutes we were headed through the wire gate. Moving west for only a thousand yards, we assembled at a clearing for a helicopter flight into the action. L.T. and Sarge were running around organizing us into groups of eight men per helicopter, making sure we had ammo, water, and radio communication with each group.

In the distance, I could hear the whoop whoop sounds of helicopter blades. In moments, small black specks appeared over the horizon. Little by little, a flight of ten Huey helicopters—in tight formation—began their descent into the clearing. We scrambled to get aboard and every man chose his spot. I sat in the middle seat; others just sat on the floor and dangled their legs out of the open doors. In seconds we were off and flying high across the jungle. I was scared, but tried not to show it. I drew my seat belt tighter around my waste. It wasn't a fear of flying that had gripped me; it was the unknown factor of what we might be flying into. A hot landing zone was a possibility, we all knew that. The VC knew that when they were in a fight with Americans, additional forces would be thrown in. Most often, they were waiting for them. Stuart Simmons, the guy from Iowa, punched me on the leg. "Open your eyes, Shorty. It's pretty down there, ain't it?" He said. He had a huge grin on his face.

"Yup, real pretty," I replied.

"I mean it, now," he said. "If you got to go somewhere, this is the way to do it. We don't have to walk through that jungle…. Feel how cool it is up here. You've just got to love it."

"Yup, real cool."

"Yeah, this is great, Shorty. I want to fly some day … maybe be a helicopter pilot."

"Yup…. Great…. You go right ahead…"

"See, we're dropping … coming in now. …looks so pretty."

I watched as the door gunners pulled the cocking levers on their machine guns. They began firing into the tree line as we began our steep plunge into the LZ. (Landing Zone). Smoke billowed from artillery fire and splintered trees lay everywhere around the small clearing. Men began jumping from the choppers while they hovered ten-to-fifteen feet off the ground. Stuart Simmons grabbed me by the shirt. "Let's go," he shouted.

We exited together. I stumbled and fell flat on my face. The choppers were gone within seconds. The other men were running toward the tree line. Stuart stood above me. "You all right, little buddy?"

"Yes, I'm OK. That jump was twice the distance for me as it was for you, but I'm OK. Thanks."

Stuart helped me up and we ran to join the rest of the company as they spread out along the wood line. We had made an uneventful landing near a heavily wooded area. It was unfamiliar to Stuart, Gary, me, and the other new guys. One man said we seldom went there and should be ready for anything.

L.T. said that in the briefing he'd received, he was told that a large NVA (North Vietnamese Army) unit had recently

First Tunnel

been seen patrolling the area. They had ambushed one of our units the day before and caused heavy casualties. We were taking their place.

"They're professionals. ...well-trained with a good supply network. Watch you step," L.T. warned. "First Platoon put up a good fight and they're out of it now. Our mission is to try to find the NVA base camp."

We groaned. This meant hours of humping through the heavy jungle. We knew they could hide forever in there and we'd be sniped at, ambushed, or worse.

After two days of crisscrossing this hot and humid jungle, we found a recently used trail. Skirting the paths so that we wouldn't leave boot marks or other signs, we followed it until late in the day. Eventually we came across a couple of well-constructed bunkers on both sides of the trail. Sarge said they were probably outposts for a base camp farther up the trail. "Keep your eyes peeled and your powder dry," he warned as he huddled in conversation with L.T.

"It's late in the day," Sarge announced after their quick meeting. "L.T. decided that we should pull back off the trail a little more and set up a perimeter for the night. At first light we'll continue to check out these sandal marks. The trail leads somewhere."

We dug in, ate our cold C-rations after dark, and even Murphy was quiet that night. Morning came all too quickly. We thought we had heard movement on the trail during the night, but we couldn't agree on exactly what it was. Still, there was no doubt that someone or something was moving out there.

At dawn, Sarge said. "Saddle up, we're moving."

We patrolled just a few meters, when someone reported they had found some bunkers. John Meddos, one of the guys who had arrived shortly before me, was selected to check out two recently constructed bunkers we had stumbled upon. They yielded nothing of value.

Meddos came crawling out of one and said, "Ain't nothing

in there but some spiders and scorpions." He removed his helmet to wipe the sweat and I observed him up close for the first time. John Meddos was completely opposite in his demeanor than what his face suggested. He was a redhead from Ohio. …Columbus, I thought I heard him say. Red freckles danced across his nose and cheeks, making him look like a teenager. Watching him, how he moved, how he was always up front, made me realize that his youthful appearance had nothing to do with his manliness. John Meddos was "all soldier" and he proved it every day. We had gone only about a thousand meters; a "click" as we called it, when the point man, Bob Tillis, yelled out: "Sarge, come here. I've found something."

"Meddos.... Mendez..." Sarge called out. "Come with me, Tillis found something."

John and I obeyed. Reluctantly, we moved forward and arrived at a set of several bunkers farther up the trail. Tillis was on one knee, rifle at the ready. He turned and motioned us to do likewise. "I heard something right up front," Tillis said. "I think I smelled fish sauce and wood smoke. We're right behind them."

Bob Tillis was another of the guys who just looked to me like they shouldn't be in the army, let alone Vietnam. He was different. Looking at his blonde hair, light complexion, and muscular build, I imagined he should be on a California beach or riding a skateboard somewhere. He had found several more bunkers and he pointed out a couple of lean-to shelters farther on. Sarge waved the rest of the men forward and carefully situated them in a semicircle. After a moment, he motioned us to move towards the enemy positions. I gulped and went forward with the others. As we approached, we began noticing plenty of evidence of recent activity. We were right behind them.

"I hope they're already gone ... left the area," I said to Tillis as I moved up to take his place on point. Soaked down to my socks with sweat, I hacked and cut at the heavy jungle

First Tunnel

brush with my machete. It was dangerous work and I knew it. The point man was always only seconds away from death if he were unlucky. Surprisingly, the difficult work relieved my anxiety. Sarge was right behind me with his weapon at the ready. When we reached the shelters, we could see that they were made of stout bamboo poles and had thatch-covered roofs.

"This is more than just a small camp," L.T. observed. "Every bunker and every path seems to lead to another bunker and another trail.

"I guess we found it. ...the base camp," I said to Sarge. "Now what do we do with it?"

It was most certainly the major base camp that we had been sent to find. But for the moment, it was empty. I sat on one of the bunkers and took a long pull from my canteen.

"I get the feeling they're close by," L.T. Said. "Tillis smelled smoke." They're sloppy ... left evidence all around. Let's move all the way in and seize the camp. We'll see what happens."

We quickly set up a protective perimeter and moved in to occupy the camp. Prudently, Lieutenant Schmitter had notified our command center of our find and asked for reinforcements in case the VC decided to return home. Headquarters agreed and said the rest of our company—three more platoons—would be airlifted to a landing zone only two clicks away, but they wouldn't join us for another four hours.

L.T. handed the radio handset to the Radio Telephone Operator (RTO). "...Captain says hold our positions and avoid any unnecessary contact until our reinforcements have landed. It'll be some time before they get here. They're about an hour away even when they land."

We nodded our understanding, held our breath and waited. Finally, Sarge gave the word to search the bunkers. Gary and I entered the dugouts and grass shelters nearest to us. They had been used regularly, and probably as recent as the day before. We found some rice in one hut. There were also cooking pots and small metal plates or skillets.

"They'll be back soon," Gary remarked as we foraged through the huts and bunkers. Nobody would abandon their supplies just like that."

"I guess they're out on patrol right about now. Let's hurry up and get out of here," I said.

Tillis joined us. He and Gary, along with some other men, agreed with my suggestion. We moved through the bunkers quickly and it was spooky as hell in there. After searching for an hour, we managed to find some propaganda leaflets but nothing of real informative value.

"You know this guy?" Stuart asked as he handed me a leaflet.

"Can't say as I do," I answered. "Who is it?"

"Uncle Ho…. Ho Chi Min, the granddaddy they're all fighting for. His message is on these leaflets. Maybe they make them here. …propaganda unit, I figure."

Murphy commented that they'd make good "ass wipe" and he stuffed his pockets with them. We settled in around the enemy base camp, waiting for our command group to hit the LZ. We took the time to prepare a late lunch for ourselves. Gary Standish and John Meddos opened cans of C-rations. I had been saving something special for a day just like this. Boiling some water over a flame made from the explosive C-4, I noticed the stuff burned like an acetylene torch.

I poured my hot water into a package of freeze-dried food. "LURP" rations, we called them. These were first developed and tested in Vietnam. They were initially issued to Long Range Recon Patrol units, hence the name "LURP" developed. After days of eating a bland and salty diet of C-rations, these dehydrated meals were delicious. They would absorb the hot water in a few minutes and the meal was ready to eat. It would hold its consistency for several hours, furnishing a hot meal when opened again. It was like magic.

My special lunch this day was beef with rice. I added a little hot sauce and had a gourmet's delight. At least that's what it meant to me at the time. After heating some water in a tin can for coffee, I had a complete meal.

We always ate quickly, as you never knew when you would be called to action and have to leave your food on the ground. In this case, in the middle of this bunker complex, we knew we'd be doing some scouting as soon as our command group called in. They'll want us to get some "results" out of those bunkers. Lunch was a secondary consideration.

Between bites, our eyes constantly searched the bushes for signs of the enemy. We didn't like to have uninvited guests. To break the tension, I teased Gary about snoring so loud the night before. He didn't believe me until John Meddos agreed: "You don't only snore, Standish, you snore with a New York accent."

We quietly chuckled and the tension eased. Finally, the Command Group called, saying they had secured their landing zone and would hurry to our area of operations.

Always the professional soldier, Sergeant Browning told us to clean up our mess. "Bury the trash deep and get your gear ready. We're going to start some widespread searches and find these prairie dogs." He sent us out in three-man groups, to a maximum of 100 feet. We were to conduct our searches, looking for anything unusual, especially bobby-traps. Mines and trip-wire explosives went hand-in-hand with a VC base camp. Sarge sent Gary and me with Larry Cunnings. He was an experienced soldier from California, and was well liked and trusted by all the guys. He told us that new guys always walk point. "They learn faster that way," he said.

We flipped a C-Ration can lid to see who would get the "honor." Gary lost. He shoved a cookie in his mouth, grabbed a machete and we moved out. We moved to our right flank, slowly poking, searching and looking at anything even remotely suspicious. We found nothing. Larry Cunnings motioned us to head back and I was relieved. It looked like the task was over and we'd be headed out of there. We were just arriving back to our perimeter when Roser said, "Hey Cunnings, they want Shorty Mendez up ahead."

I looked at Roser, quizzing him. "Why me? What's up, Roser?"

He noticed my apprehension and replied, "Oh, nothing big. I think they found a tunnel or something and want to put your short butt down the hole." My heart stopped.

"Are you for real?"

"Yeah," he said. "They've been grooming you to be our 'tunnel rat.' I heard them talking."

Roser and I walked about 75 feet and joined the forward search team. They had found more bunkers and a woven mat that covered a hole in the ground. As I approached, several of the men were looking tentatively into the hole, but avoided being directly over it. I didn't have to ask why, and I figured if they were that cautious, I would be even more wary.

Sergeant Browning looked my way. "You ever been down a hole before, Private Mendez?"

"Well, ah, er, they did give me a little search training at Fort Polk. I've never been in a real one."

He handed me his .45-caliber automatic pistol and a flashlight.

"You're our official tunnel rat now," Sergeant Browning said. "You'll go down in a minute after the C.O. (Commanding Officer) and his group gets here. Shed some of that gear; you won't need it down there."

I sat mesmerized, a few feet from the tunnel entrance. I couldn't believe I would soon be underground, looking and crawling through a tunnel for who knew what?

What would I do if someone were down there?

Sweat poured down my back and into my underwear. (Maybe it was sweat.) My heart raced and my mind envisioned all kinds of things: *What if I get stuck down there? Is there enough air? Do snakes and bugs live underground? Why wasn't I born a six-foot gorilla?*

First Tunnel

Sarge interrupted my thoughts. He was leading the Company Commander and Lieutenant Schmitter. Captain Stiles asked if I was all set.

"Yes, Sir. Ready as I'll ever be, I guess," I said.

"It'll be OK, Private Mendez. You just watch your step and back out of there if you spot anything. You're not going down to fight ... just look around. We'll back you up. If anything happens we'll be right there."

I wondered who would be right there. I looked at the hole again. I didn't know of anyone except me who could fit through it. "Thanks, Sir," I said.

Captain Stiles was an efficient commander. I trusted him and his words made me feel better. He turned and instructed the men to set up a tight perimeter. He told them I was going down and he asked for volunteers to go down if I needed help.

"I'll go," Gary said without hesitation. "Right now, I'll stand in the opening in case he needs anything."

"Good man," Captain Stiles said. Sarge and L.T. nodded in agreement.

"OK... down you go," Sarge ordered.

I was stripping my gear and looking over the .45-caliber pistol and checking the flashlight. I looked at Gary.

"Do you think you might need me? I'm too big for that little hole," Gary said.

"Why the heck did you tell them you'd come get me if you're unsure? Damn... Gary."

Gary grinned. "Oh, I don't know... seemed like a good idea at the time. Don't worry, I'll be there."

"You just wanted to look good in front of the Captain. That's it, isn't it?"

"No."

"Then why did you say you'd go down?"

Gary blushed: "'Cause you're my brother.... I can't let anything happen to you. I'll be there."

I was moved by Gary's remark. I couldn't think of an

appropriate reply. Brothers? I guess we had become that.

"Just in case I chase some bad guys out, you can catch them in your arms and be a hero," I said.

"Cool..." Gary pointed towards the hole. "You go now ... and good luck, little buddy."

I slid my hand around the inside of the opening, feeling for bobby traps. I didn't touch anything, so I slowly crawled in; headfirst. The flashlight wasn't as bright as I hoped, but I could see fairly well. The tunnel was a little wider than shoulder width for maybe three feet, then it widened up to about two-feet across by about four-feet high. I could almost stand. I paused for a moment in the larger tunnel. My breathing was very fast and my eyes were slowly adjusting to the dark. I couldn't see anything for the first 30 seconds. I sat there for a few minutes to adjust my eyes and listen.

The air was heavy and musty and it smelled like mold. The surrounding earth was moist and it was very cool to the touch. In fact, I felt relief from the heat and humidity just a few feet above me. Oddly, I felt comfortable down there. I realized that the folks above couldn't tell if I was searching or not. I could just sit there for 20 minutes, then crawl out and tell them I'd found nothing. But, what if there was something?

I couldn't hear any noises, so I moved forward in a modified duck walk. I searched every inch of the way, feeling with my hands in front of me and along the walls. I was looking for trip wires and bobby traps. At about fifteen feet down the tunnel, it made a sharp left turn. I slowly peered around the turn and froze! I saw two bare feet disappearing into the wall of the tunnel. *Is that another tunnel, or did I imagine I saw feet?*

I was really hyped up now. *Should I go ahead?* I was getting farther and farther from my friends topside.

Would that VC get away and alert the rest of his fellow soldiers? Would our guys get caught by surprise?

I swallowed hard and decided to crawl forward. I wiggled within a foot of where the feet had disappeared. Lying on my

First Tunnel

belly, I stretched forward with my flashlight and meekly reached into the opening. With the hammer cocked on my pistol, I flicked on the light with my right thumb. Nothing happened. I took a very quick glance around the corner and saw no one. I proceeded to crawl into this new tunnel, which was no tunnel at all, but rather a large room. It measured about fifteen by twenty feet. I quickly surveyed the dark room and could see a low table and some boxes stacked, one on top of the other. There were about ten of them. Behind the boxes, where I expected to find the VC hiding, was another hole. I was really getting nervous and it was especially hard for me to breath. I lit up the new hole with the flashlight and noticed that it angled upward. I looked up and could see dim rays of light coming from above.

In the glare of that faint light, I could see the VC escaping out of the tunnel. It was a mistake. If he had remained still, I might have missed him. Without hesitation, I fired two quick rounds up into the shaft. In an instant, I found myself sitting on my butt holding my head in pain from the horrendous blast. A .45-caliber pistol has a really big bang, but it is ten times as loud underground. The rancid, choking smoke from the two rounds made me cough violently. I needed air and light and friendship. I decided to get out of there.

As fast as possible, I made my way back to the main tunnel where I could see light from my entrance hole. In a frenzy, almost blind from the dirt and sweat, I reached for the opening. Gary grabbed my arm and quickly pulled me out of the hole.

I lay at the lip of the opening, breathing hard and shaking. As I lay there, Gary talked to me, asking me questions and trying to calm me down. I could see Captain Stiles and L.T. running forward into the woods.

"Hey, little buddy, you did good," Gary said. "The outer perimeter guys caught a wounded VC running like hell. Roser said he was shot in the ass. You must have winged him. What happened down there?"

I looked at Standish. "I can't hear a word you're saying... the noise... my head..." Actually, I could hear slightly, but everything seemed like an echo. Sarge came running to where I lay catching my breath. Through my gasps, I explained how I fired at the escaping VC and how bad my head hurt.

"But, I'll bet his butt hurts worse than my head right about now," I said.

Sarge smiled and said I had done an excellent job. "What did you see down there?"

"It looked like a storage area for equipment. It's a big room with boxes stacked up to the ceiling."

"What's in 'em?" Sarge asked.

"I didn't have a chance to check them," I said. "After I fired at the VC, I just had to get out of there."

"You did good, "Mr. Tunnel Rat," Sarge said, and he beamed at me.

He turned to Gary. "Go down there and check those boxes, Standish. Tunnel Rat has cleared the way. ...shouldn't be no problem." Gary turned beet red. Silently he stripped himself of his gear, grabbed the light and the pistol. He blessed himself, took a breath, and headed down into the darkness. I was glad to have the time to rest my head and my nerves.

"When Standish gets back up, you keep that pistol and light," Sarge said. "There are lots of tunnels in Vietnam. You make good use of that 45."

I looked up and a few men had gathered around me. Big Murphy reached into one of his side pockets.

"Have a beer, Tunnel Rat. You earned it. I gotta get back."

He shoved it into my hand, turned and headed for the front. It was almost cold—a Budweiser. I wondered how he could produce cold beer in the middle of the jungle. I wondered why he had made the gesture. It was a turning point for me in my combat career. I had proved something to myself and to the men in our platoon. I was proud and I think I even grew an inch or two that afternoon.

First Tunnel

From that day on, I was known as, "Tunnel Rat." Seldom did anyone in my platoon call me Shorty after that.

Doc Bob Barult, a broad shouldered Georgia boy was our platoon medic. His broad reddish mustache was always well groomed from his constant twisting of the ends.

"How do you feel, Tunnel Rat? Any problems?" he said.

"I'm Okay... just a little headache."

"Can't have our rat feeling bad. Here's a couple of aspirin. Drink a lot of water. Need something stronger, ask me."

"Thanks, Doc." I closed my eyes.

"Hey, Mendez, are you still there?" Simmons shouted into the phone. I jumped up from my easy chair and simultaneously from that bunker. His booming voice had brought me back to reality.

"Yeah, Hayseed, but I'm going down memory lane, right now."

"Well, save all that memory for the reunion. Do you think you can make it?"

"I wouldn't miss it for all the MPC (Military Payment Certificates) in Vietnam. Just send me all the details and I'll be there," I assured him.

"It will be great to have all the guys together again," Stuart said. "See you then."

I hung up the phone, still half dazed at the flood of memories flowing in my mind. There was even an echo in my ears.

IV

COUNTER ATTACK

I sat silently for a while after Stuart's voice faded, watching a blank TV screen.

"Who was that?" my wife asked. "You Okay? You seem to be in a world of your own."

"Sorry, Honey. Just some guy I used to know. ...Took me back a ways."

Closing my eyes, I went right back to that first tunnel. My mind was swamped with the memory of that particular experience and all of the events that followed.

The VC I had shot in the butt had been captured. He was surround by a group of "rubber necker's" and guys kept coming up to see him. A captured enemy soldier was a rare experience, and I, just like the others, went to look at him. Captain Stiles was obviously in charge and had just finished tying his hands behind his back. Doc Barult was cleaning and bandaging his wound. Someone offered water. These displays of compassion affected me and I began to feel sorry for the boy. He was shaking like a leaf; frightened to death to be in our hands. He was even smaller than me and looked to be about sixteen or seventeen years old.

"He doesn't look so tough now, does he? Stuart said. "We should keep him as a pet."

I nodded. I was wishing I was somewhere else, away from this war. "He's just a kid, a little boy," I said

Sergeant Browning had overheard us. "Yeah, a little boy with an AK-47 rifle in his hands will kill you as quick as an old man. Remember that."

Counter Attack

Our Vietnamese interpreter was jabbering, gesturing menacingly, and pointing his pistol at our prisoner from time to time. Someone else was rummaging through his backpack. It held some writing paper, a diary, and pictures of an older woman and some children. Rice balls wrapped in banana leaves littered the ground and I figured those were his rations.

Sergeant Dong (Don) a member of the South Vietnamese Army, but assigned to us as an interpreter, conducted the interrogation. In spite of his efforts, our prisoner revealed nothing of value. He gave only his name, rank and serial number, just as he had been trained to do. We learned nothing about his unit—any clues as to where they had gone—or how long before they might return. Sergeant Dong cocked his pistol and pointed it at the prisoner's head. He yelled some unintelligible command and I held my breath in anticipation of the impending execution.

"Whoa!" Captain Stiles shouted as he held up his hand and stepped between Sergeant Dong and the prisoner. "Put your pistol away, we don't shoot prisoners."

Sergeant Dong smiled and obeyed, explaining that he was only using scare tactics to try prying information from the prisoner. "I would not break the rules," he said. His mood soured then, and he turned toward the group. "I can get nothing from him. You Americans are too gentle toward our enemy. He is a communist! You will come to regret that we did not learn from him. I am finished. Give him cookies and milk ... that is your way, No?"

Before anyone could answer, we heard the faint sounds of mortars leaving their tubes. "Incoming!" Sarge yelled. He didn't have to say it twice. We scattered like cockroaches when the lights come on. Gary and I dove into a nearby bunker. Within seconds they hit: "Whomp, whomp, whomp!" I can still hear that frightening sound. Clearly, the enemy had figured out we were in their base camp. They were preparing to counter attack, beginning with a barrage of mortar fire. I was sure a ground assault would follow.

Our prisoner had been left in the open with Sergeant Dong. The first few rounds killed both of them instantly. There was little left of either soldier. Afterward, we found only the dead VC's papers, scattered about the base camp like so much confetti. I picked up one of his pictures. "Probably his family," I said to Gary.

As quickly as they began, the mortar rounds stopped. Small arms and machine gun fire erupted to our front and on the right flank. We hugged the ground to conceal ourselves and prepared to shoot it out. Luckily, L.T. and Captain Stiles had established a shrewd perimeter of our men and weapons. He had a plan for artillery support and our Forward Observer was on the radio calling it in.

Sarge was shouting directions for us to, "fire like hell," and fire we did. We could see the enemy moving in on us; methodically advancing by leaps and bounds through the brush. They were a large unit, obviously well trained and brave. Our superior firepower slowed them, but they kept on coming. We were in their home and they were determined to take it back. They attacked again and again. Each time it seemed as if the barrage of bullets was letting up, they would attack in full force again.

L.T. shouted that artillery was on its way and we should keep our heads down. Within minutes high explosive shells hit the heavy canopy of the jungle in front of us. White-hot shrapnel came zinging through the trees, bouncing off the earthen bunkers in which we sought protection.

Mentally, I thanked the VC for building them. When it came to artillery, there was no distinction between friend and foe. The forward observer had to keep it off us and on the VC. In this case, he was right on target. Rounds were landing one right after the other and we quivered from the heavy vibrations as they slammed into the earth. Everything shook and showers of earth splashed over us.

Counter Attack

Running low on ammunition, I knew I had to pick my targets well. Gary and I spotted two VC within a few feet of our position and heaved grenades into their midst. The sounds of battle increased. Our machine guns on either flank were doing their work. Their methodical bursts of six rounds at a time told me that our guys were fighting "smart." The artillery shells boomed, crashing only a few yards in front of us now, and caught the attacking enemy in the open. Still they kept coming.

"You hear that?" Gary said, He was calm and in control of his emotions.

"What?" I asked

"We're going to be OK … I hear chopper blades … gunships coming."

"Hope they hurry, I'm almost out of ammo."

"Me too. I checked my pack and I only have two cookies left. Want one? Better fix bayonets."

I did both. The cookie was a welcome distraction, and my bayonet snapped into place with a loud click. I wondered if I'd have to use it. Two Cobra gunships appeared overhead. They had come in with machine guns blazing and didn't waste time circling. The intensity of fire slackened and the enemy began to withdraw. The firepower was too much for them.

We could hear a chopper landing somewhere in the rear and soon men were bringing up ammunition. I reloaded, took a drink of water, and relaxed. It appeared to be over.

By late afternoon, patrols had verified that the enemy had totally withdrawn. Dead bodies were collected and buried. We had several wounded, but no one killed. We were proud of our achievement, but there is a quiet regret that hangs in every man's soul after a fierce battle where men fight and die. There was little joy for me or for anyone in this victory.

Squads of men began to discuss the battle and its meaning. Why had the enemy squandered their lives against such superior firepower? I wondered.

Larry Cunnings, Bob Tillis, and John Meddos told us how they had crawled and dodged bullets, diving into a bunker at my left. They had been near the prisoner and interpreter when the mortars first hit.

"Hey, Rat," Murphy said. "You get any of them? I saw those grenades come flying."

I feigned ignorance and looked around for a huge rat. "Where's the rat?" I said. "We have rats?" The jungles of Vietnam were home to some very large rodents and every G.I. had heard stories about these rats. We were always on guard for them.

"You, Shorty. You're the rat... Tunnel Rat Number One!" You FNGs did good for your first fight. I got a chance to blow some sorry-ass VCs to hell. You know you caused it all, don't you, Rat?"

"Who, Me?"

"Sure. See, I figure they wanted their prisoner back real bad or they wanted what's in that tunnel you searched. They could have moved and built a base camp anywhere."

Lieutenant Schmitter came up and talked with us for a while. He commended us on our performance and then made the same observation as Murphy.

"I think they wanted that tunnel. You guys agree?"

He questioned Murphy, Cunnings and Tillis, asking how hard the enemy in front of them had fought. Cunnings said that he agreed: To him, it seemed they wanted the tunnel very bad.

"They were putting heavy machine gun fire all around the opening area of that tunnel during the fight," he said.

Sarge came up and said he needed Tunnel Rat, Standish and Roser. We quickly followed him expecting to search out to our front. Lieutenant Schmitter looked at us, obviously concerned, but he spoke directly: "Sarge is taking you three back to the tunnel. Mendez, you'll go down again. I need to know what you didn't see. Maybe there are some papers, weapons... who knows what? Seems like they wanted something in there."

Sarge piped in. "Yeah, they wouldn't risk their whole unit just for a few bunkers and a small tunnel complex. Be sharp, look around real good down there. Standish, you follow him. This time, go all the way. Roser and I will secure the opening while you two search. I'll put more men around your perimeter. They might have the grit to attack us again, so don't waste time."

That we had almost lost the battle never occurred to me. Yes, the enemy had gained ground to within a few yards of us, but with our artillery and aerial support, the outcome was never in doubt. Several prisoners were taken in the melee, and after-action reports revealed how close we were to losing it. One prisoner told us what their objective had been.

*T*he provincial leader of that area, Colonel Nyen Toi, was the commander of the VC unit that had built the base camp and attacked us. While we were entering his camp and searching the tunnel, he was hastily arranging his forces for an attack. He told his unit leaders that at all costs, the sensitive documents in those boxes had to be retrieved. The loss of these papers would completely compromise the infrastructure of local Viet Cong and destroy his control over the civilian population in his area, he told them.

"These documents list our staging plans, locations of arms caches and our transport routes," he told his soldiers. "They have the names of unit leaders and the names of double-agents working with the Americans. These papers must not fall into their hands. Attack the Americans, kill them all! Take back your land! In the new Vietnam, you will be honored as heroes whether you live or die. My own nephew—my only living flesh and blood—volunteered to stay behind and protect our cache. He has pledged to die for our cause. You must do everything to rescue him. You must destroy the Americans and the tunnel," Colonel Nyen Toi commanded.

Gary appeared nervous. Nevertheless, he followed me, forcing his shoulders through the narrow opening. "I don't fit very well," he said. "Guess I should go tell Sarge."

I looked back at him: "Get your fat ass in here with me. You'll do OK if you can crawl to the larger tunnel. I'll do the rest from there."

Gary wiggled some more and we made it to the larger tunnel. He wasn't eager to go much farther. When he was excited, he breathed loud and fast. This time he sounded like a steam engine.

"You stay right here, Gary," I said. "Listen for my call if I need you or if we need Sarge. I'll take another quick look in the large room and be right back."

His eyes as big as fruit melons, he nodded his agreement. I began my crawl. At the turn in the tunnel, I shined the flashlight into the opening of the larger room. I crawled through and shined the light around, trying to see if I might have overlooked something the first time. There were only those wooden boxes in the corner. I hadn't opened them the first time as I was interrupted by the fleeing VC soldier. I studied them and didn't see anything different. They hadn't been disturbed. Even so, I shuffled over to them and checked lightly with my free hand for any wires or something that might indicate a booby-trap. The enemy enjoyed putting grenades or other types of explosives in, on, or around objects they wished to protect. They often killed or maimed the careless or untrained soldier. I'd heard stories about men who were blown up trying to retrieve objects they thought would be a great souvenir.

Holding my breath, I carefully pulled the lid from the top box. It was full of papers: just folders of papers with Vietnamese writing and figures. In training, I had learned that if something looked important, it usually was. I stuffed handfuls of documents in my shirt and trousers pockets, and then scooted out of there, back to where Gary waited.

"Man, I'm glad to see you," he said. "I didn't believe a

place could be so dark and make me feel so helpless."

"Yup, I feel that way all the time down here. I'm not really a rat ... have no instinct for it. Here, take these papers up to Sarge and see if we need to bring the rest. The boxes would be real tight getting through this part of the tunnel. I can't imagine how they got them in here. Tell Sarge there are three boxes of the stuff. Hurry up and come back ... bring me a cookie."

"Certainly," Gary said. He didn't hesitate and was out of sight in seconds. Time moved in slow motion as I awaited Gary's return. I rested in the pitch black with my back against the tunnel wall. Moist dirt dropped down the back of my shirt and it felt as if it was crawling. I was sure a spider or something worse was now working its way down to my shorts. I sat absolutely still, waiting to see if I'd be stung. Nothing happened.

Finally I heard, "Hey, Shorty, it's me. I'm coming back down. Don't shoot"

Falling dirt hit my face and mouth as he slid into dim view. I spit it out, and looked in his direction. My eyes were now very accustomed to the dark and I could see him; but he couldn't see me very well.

"Well, were they worth anything or what?" I said.

"What?" Was what worth anything?"

"The papers, you goofball!"

"Oh, them? Yeah, Sarge said it was a good find ... bring it all up." I was just teasing you. Here's your lunch." He handed me a cookie, which I put in my pocket.

You've got to love the guy.

"You'll have to help," I told Gary. "If we work together, we can get it all in one trip."

"Then let's do it quick and get the hell out of here? I have claustrophobia or something. Did I ever tell you about my coal-miner father? Remind me to tell you the story some day."

I shuttle-walked and Gary crawled. We made our way back to the main room. He stayed close as I shined my flashlight on the boxes.

"Let's get what's in these boxes and get topside," I said. "Stuff it in every nook and cranny you have." Suddenly, the ground began to shake and shudder. Dirt and dust began to fall from the inside walls of the tunnel complex.

"Earthquake," Gary said. "I read about them. Or it might be mortar fire. Same damn thing ... we're trapped."

I looked at him for a second, and then drew the same conclusion. We had incoming mortar fire and maybe enemy contact above ground. I hadn't heard about any earthquakes in Vietnam.

"Move it," I yelled. We shoved papers in our shirts, in our pockets, and anywhere we had an opening in our clothing. Gary had two handfuls and even some in his mouth, but we got them all. As we turned to crawl back out, loud bursts of small arms fire cracked loudly. The tunnel walls began to crumble and hit us with small showers of dirt. Several VC were entering through the same hole where I had wounded the fleeing VC earlier that day. My heart went into my throat.

Gary rolled to one side, raising the M-16 he had dragged down the tunnel with him. I turned and fired my .45- caliber pistol as Gary let loose a hail of bullets. Two enemy soldiers fell and another retreated through the exit. It was as if someone instantly turned off the sound, I couldn't hear anything for a few moments. I looked at Gary and saw blood oozing from his pant leg.

"You hurt bad?"

He answered, but I couldn't understand a word of it. It looked like he had been grazed along the thigh. Gary frantically waved his hands telling me that he wanted to get out of there. I didn't argue and we started for the main opening. I motioned Gary to crawl out first and I would pick up the papers we had dropped and hand them through. Our men were waiting and they jerked Gary out of the hole. I popped my head and arms out and Roser pulled me the rest of the way.

"No time for small talk," Roser yelled as he pointed toward

our rear. Let's go!"

With Gary already yards ahead of us, we ran for about one hundred meters and found our platoon set up in a protective perimeter. I slammed down in a small depression in the earth. Roser joined me with Gary taking a spot nearby.

"Medic!" He cried.

"What's happening? I asked Roser.

"We took incoming mortar fire not long after you went down," Roser said. They're at it again. Fools!"

I waived my hands and pointed to my ears. "I can't hardly hear you, I said, but I have the idea." The ringing in my ears was maddening at first, but now lessening in intensity. I could bear it. The headaches would come later.

Doc Barult was putting a bandage on Gary's leg. He grimaced as Doc applied an antiseptic. Doc was asking questions, but Gary just couldn't answer; he couldn't hear anything either. I crawled over and put my hand on his shoulder. He looked at me for a moment and then gave the universal thumbs up sign. His lips said, "Thanks, Buddy."

I patted his shoulder to indicate I felt the same.

Smiling, he made a fist and shook it at me. I laughed. We were speaking volumes to each other without the use of words. Only real friends can do that.

We had no more contact with Colonel Nyen Toi's Viet Cong that day. One of our sister units joined us later and we were "beefed up" as Sarge put it. The next day, after a thorough search of the bunkers, engineers packed the few remaining bunkers and "my" tunnel with explosives. Most of them had been destroyed by artillery and mortar fire, but the final explosions would ensure that nothing of value would be left for the enemy.

"Mission accomplished," L.T. said. "Let's go home."

We returned to our base camp for several days of rest and to rearm. Lieutenant Schmitter came by to let us know the boxes of papers we had recovered were very important.

Our Headquarters was already using the information against local VC units. One very interesting document from that cache was the unit roster. It contained the names of the men under Colonel Nyen Toi's command.

Intelligence analysts had determined that the Colonel had a nephew under his command. L.T. suggested that maybe he planned to keep his family under his wing during the war. "It would have been a nice catch, if we had captured that nephew," he said.

I strung my hammock. The Colonel had his agenda and I had mine. "Gary, hand me a beer," I said as I stretched out in the cool shade." I was only interested in enjoying the down time, not thinking about Colonel Nyen Toi, his nephew, or the war. We spent the remainder of our time off grilling steaks, drinking beer, playing cards, and, oh, yes, occasionally munching on oatmeal cookies. ...Ah, the good times.

VI

ASSEMBLY

*M*y hotel arrangements were made and my bags were packed. I had spent several afternoons and evenings digging through trunks to round up my old photo albums. I wanted to take remembrances and souvenirs for the fellows to see. Sitting down on one of the trunks, I turned the pages of one special album. Halfway through, I stopped browsing; I had found what I didn't know I was looking for.

We had taken one group photo of all the guys in our platoon in Vietnam and I sent a copy home. As I stared at it, my mind slowly filled with more memories. Memories I hated, but memories I also cherished. I stared at the faces of young men dressed in combat fatigues, with rifles or machine guns in their hands and bandoleers of ammunition strung around their waists. There was Gary... so young, so strong, and so innocent. In fact, they were all young, strong and blameless for whatever caused that war, whatever actions they took to stay alive.

"America's finest," I said. These men had become like brothers to me. Their faces would never fade from my memory. I couldn't remember all of their names but their features were as fresh as yesterday. I vowed to recall every name in that group before the reunion, if I could. I wondered if they would remember me. Thirty years might have likewise erased their ability to recall names, to remember those times, but I was sure they felt like me. Together, we had experienced something few men on this earth will ever know or feel. We were combat veterans who had lived, fought, and suffered beside each other. Some of those in the photo had not been so lucky, they didn't come home. We survivors had made it home because we had pulled together. Yes, we were all brothers then, and the passing years couldn't change that. We were brothers now.

"How are you doing, Honey? Lost down memory lane?"

Linda, my very supportive and loving wife, had sneaked up on me. She knew some things about Vietnam, but we had never fully explored the entire experience. Like most veterans, I just didn't want to talk much about it. Like most veterans, I had blocked out much of the war. Still it lay rooted in my soul and the men were ever-present in my heart. Sometimes at night I would wake up thinking I was trapped in a tunnel. My cold sweats and groaning startled Linda each time. Without comment, one day she brought a special light for our bedroom. In twenty-years I can't remember changing the bulb. I guess she does that.

"Yeah, Linda, you got me. I was lost there for a minute. Do you need me to cut the grass or something?" I closed the album.

"No, you cut it yesterday. I just wanted you to know that I understand. You go to this reunion and make something of it. It'll be good for you."

"Yes, it'll be good..."

"Next time I'll go along. You're still too good looking for me to let you out of my sight for very long." With a chuckle and a soft kiss, Linda left me to my thoughts.

If I was blocking it out, it would soon come rushing back. That phone call from Stuart Simmons was only the beginning, I knew. The upcoming reunion would, on the surface, be filled with good times and laughter. Beneath the hilarity, each of us would be looking for the answers to questions that were always nagging. Long hidden emotions and contradictory feelings about the whole thing tugged at my soul and at theirs, I was sure. I was, at the same time, eager to see the guys, but hesitant to relive the stories of our time in Vietnam.

"What if?" I said to no one. "Why...?" I wondered if any

of my real close friends would come to the reunion. Gary Standish? I had thought little about him lately and regretted that. Roser? I should have asked Stuart Simmons. I wonder if big Murphy is still around? I hate the thought that any one of them might have died before we could have a reunion.

I went to the kitchen. "I don't know, maybe I won't go."

"What?" Linda asked. "Won't go? I don't believe you. You'll go. You look at those pictures more intently than you look at our own family photographs. These men are your other family. Maybe you only knew them for a year, but something happened during that year. You'll go if I have to drag you there myself."

She was right; I would go because these men were once my family. When you live with each other for a year—it seemed like an eternity then—you develop a bond. We held a sacred faith of sorts. Sacred because back then, we trusted each other with something we would trust no other man with: we trusted each other with our lives. Some men might come to the reunion out of curiosity, and some because they still feel patriotic. But it was that connection—believing in one another—that would bring me back from Vietnam and to this reunion. I grabbed Linda's soft waist from behind. "I was just kidding. I'll go. I wanted to give you the chance to tell me not to go."

"Liar. You're afraid to take this step, but I can understand it. Just go and have a good time. You'll never know what might come of it later."

Many couples, after years of marriage, can almost tell what the other person is thinking. Linda was better than that. I often thought she was psychic, could read my mind and tell the future. I trusted her judgment implicitly.

"OK, I'm out of here on Wednesday. I hope the plane doesn't crash."

"Mother Mary, give me patience…" Linda slapped me with a towel. We hugged and laughed.

Coming out of Tampa, my plane was right on time.

Finally high above the clouds, a pretty flight attendant approached to tell me I could relax and, "remove your grip from the arm rests, Sir."

"Just checking the quality of the appointments," I said.

"Humm.... Would you like a cocktail, Mr. Mendez?"

"Sure, I don't drink. But maybe a beer... you have beer?

"Yes, we have beer. Do you have a choice of brands?"

"Yes, Bourbon... Jack Daniels. A double... no, a triple."

"Ok, Mr. Mendez. We'll make it a double whiskey.

She smiled and left to prepare my drink.

I'm loosing it. What is this; a newfound fear of flying?

After the army, after 'Nam, I had overcome any angst about being in a plane or a chopper. Like Stuart said back then: "Isn't it great?"

I wouldn't admit it to anyone, but it was the anticipation of seeing my old friends that made me grip the armrests so tightly.

Imagine if I walk in there and for four days nobody knows me or even speaks to me. What if I made somebody mad back then? Murphy...? There was that time I put the dead snake in his rucksack....

My sweet flight attendant returned with my drink. She tied it with a napkin and took my hand, wrapping my fingers around the glass. She held it there for just a second, then asked: "You're a Vietnam Veteran, aren't you?"

"Wow. Yes, how did you know?"

"Oh, it's something I've learned to see in men. My father was a Vietnam Veteran. It's in the eyes, I think."

"In the eyes? What do you see in mine?"

"Well, my father had this far away look all the time. He told us kids he was looking for the light at the end of the tunnel, whatever that meant."

"I know what he meant."

"Where are you going, Mr. Mendez? I have a minute. May I sit down?"

I thought of Linda. "Why sure... no harm there. I'm headed

to a reunion of my old unit from Vietnam. It's my first time."

"My dad would go every year. He enjoyed his time with his friends. After reunions, we could talk to him about it more and he'd tell us things. It isn't easily explained, but if you looked into the eyes of my dad, or in the eyes of any veteran, you would see it there. These men made history the hard way. Reunions always took my dad back to his youth and he could feel the emotions of combat once again."

"Wow, Your dad was quite a guy. I've never told my kids very much."

"I always tell our Vietnam Veterans how proud we are of them." My father taught us that. You guys didn't have much of a homecoming."

"You have that right.... When was your father in Vietnam?"

"I can't remember exactly. He'd tell so many stories. He's gone now ... passed away last year.

"Aw, gee. I'm sorry for your loss. What did he die of? So young…"

"Cirrhosis of the liver. He drank himself to death. Look, it's been nice talking to you. Here's a newspaper and some magazines. Enjoy your flight."

Nobody would believe this conversation. Shorty, you have to write a book someday.

I took that day's newspaper and settled into my seat to read and enjoy the flight. The bourbon had helped. The regular news was not of much interest, but a small article in the "Who's Who" section caught my eye: "Vietnam Soldier Makes Goodwill Tour," the banner read. I usually read anything that has to do with Vietnam, but there is still a small sense of regret over the whole affair. I chose my literature carefully. The press hadn't done us much good when we were over there. This article was upbeat, however. It said that a representative of the government of Vietnam was traveling the United States to help restore good relations.

In quoting the gentleman, the article said that he

"understands how the people of America feel about the war."

He had also served his country in that same war for North Vietnam. As a commander of a small unit in South Vietnam, he said he was very familiar with the U.S. armed forces that served west of "Ho Chi Minh City." I grimaced at the title—it was called Saigon when I was there.

Reading further, I learned that he too, had suffered from the tragedy of war. He had lost some of his family to American soldiers. I sympathized for a moment. Most people forget that the other side, whatever their beliefs, feel the pain and sorrow of war, also. The article explained that as an older man, he understood now, how Americans thought about war and how they valued life. He was impressed at how we honor our war dead. He had just visited Arlington National Cemetery and The Vietnam Veterans Memorial in Washington. He was being sponsored on his tour by a Washington based "good will group" the paper said. By coincidence, his next stop coincided with our reunion. He was to speak to a civic group in Nashville, Tennessee; the same city where our reunion was being held.

It sure as heck is a small world, I thought, as I closed my eyes and dozed. The drink and the hum of the engines were relaxing. Besides, I would need my rest. As I remember our guys, they used to stay up late to "party" when we had the chance in base camp. We were older now, but I was certain that our youthful exuberance was still alive. What was it the flight attendant said? "Reunions always took my dad back to his youth." I would need the rest just to keep up with them.

The plane jerked as the wheels hit the runway. On the second bounce I came fully awake. The Nashville terminal flashed by the window and the airplane brakes screeched loudly. We were thrust forward against our seatbelts. I thought I heard "Oops" over the intercom. Must be a rookie, I thought.
No Vietnam pilot would make a landing that bad.

We docked at the terminal and exited, each soul headed to a new destination, a new experience. I hadn't been on a plane

Assembly

in years or moved through crowds at a terminal. Nashville reminded me of our landing in Vietnam. Like the terminal at Ton Son Nhut, this lobby was a jungle of people hurriedly going in their own directions. The only difference was there were no flares to light the sky, no cannons booming, no Super Saber fighters shattering the air overhead. It was an uncertain future I faced in Vietnam. This time I knew where I was going.

I collected my baggage and went to the hotel shuttle waiting area. There, I met an older couple on their fiftieth wedding anniversary vacation. They hoped to see the Grand Ole Opry and ride on a riverboat. That's why people usually come to Nashville: to see the tourist attractions, listen to the music, and experience the flavor of the South. I congratulated them on their years of marriage, but told them I had come for different reasons. He was a WW II Veteran and immediately understood.

We shook hands and then I noticed a man standing just outside the waiting area. There was no reason for me to speak or introduce myself, so I shuffled my feet and hummed a couple of bars of the Army Song. It is strange how tunes pop into your head and won't go away.

I had no reason to be watching this man, except that I was (probably subconsciously) looking for someone from my platoon. This fellow was average in height, slightly bald and was fighting a little weight problem. I pondered the changes that I had gone through over the years. *Would anyone recognize me without my wearing one of the infamous pin-on nametags you see at business conventions? Guess my short size will be a little hint of who I might be.*

I noticed the man seemed edgy and he kept checking his watch. He looked lost. Eventually he entered the shuttle waiting area and took a seat. "Shuttle on time?" he asked, looking directly at me.

He looks familiar.... No, I don't know this man. Still.... I cleared my head. "I'm really not sure," I said. "I just got here. The bulletin says it should arrive on the hour so we have about another ten minutes."

"You here on business?" he asked.

"No, I'm guessing I'm here for pleasure. I haven't seen the people I'll be visiting for some thirty years or so. I'm hoping it'll be pleasurable."

His eyes brightened. He stood up and smiled. "Hot dog! You're here for the Charlie Company reunion, huh?"

"Why, yes. Don't tell me you were in Charlie Company, too?"

"Hell, yeah!" He extended his hand and I took it. We were both excited and relieved to find someone so quickly who may have been a close buddy: at least a member of Charlie Company.

"Are you staying at the Roman Inn?" he asked.

"I'll be there for the rest of the week," I said. "By the way, my name is Mendez. They used to call me Shorty."

"Damn, Damn, Damn, I remember you! You were the company tunnel rat. My name's Tillis ... Bob Tillis. It' so good to see you, Shorty." He shook my hand again.

"Yes, I think I remember you, Bob. It's been a while. You hung around with Roser most of the time. Weren't you the assistant machine gunner with Dave Whiteman?

"Yeah, Whiteman. I remember him. He was tough little guy... from down south somewhere"

"You sure got me pegged right off," Bob Tillis said. "I hope the rest of the guys are easy to recognize as you."

I would never have guessed his name on sight alone. The shuttle came into view, stopped efficiently at our feet, and we boarded with great expectations. We arrived at the hotel and walked through the lobby to the front desk, looking left and right for other Vietnam veterans who might be there. I recognized no one. The check-in was quick and efficient. The clerk smiled and welcomed us as members of Charlie Company, giving us advice as to where our group would meet later. I got the feeling that our get-together was well organized. I flashed back to a time when Vietnam veterans were not greeted so warmly.

Assembly

I turned to Bob Tillis with a thousand images of the past flashing through my mind. "Bob, did you hear that desk clerk? He said welcome home—"

"About time, don't you think?" Bob said. "I'm in room 602. My schedule says they've set aside a waterin' hole for us. ...hospitality room. Will I see you there tonight? They've arranged for drinks and snacks."

"Wouldn't miss it," I assured him. I planned to get a little rest and then check to see who else might have arrived. I was getting into the spirit of the event and suddenly felt glad that I had come. The reluctance I had initially felt about coming was passing and I knew why: It was the flight attendant; the clerk; the old couple; Bob Tillis....

My room was neat and clean. I dropped my bags and tried the mattress, laying my head against the soft pillow. *Things sure are different today. ... might try on my old uniform when I get back home. I wonder where my brass is....* A loud ringing jarred me from my nap and I fumbled for the phone. "Hello."

"Mr. Mendez, your presence is requested in the reunion hospitality room." The phone went dead before I could reply. A smile creased my face; I couldn't help it. There was a faint familiarity to the voice although I couldn't place it. It delighted me that someone from the gang was looking for "Mr. Mendez." I hurriedly cleaned up and headed to the hospitality room. Never too early for a little socializing, I thought.

Hesitating for a moment at the open door, I checked faces before entering the hospitality room, trying to recognize someone from the past. The room fell silent and all heads turned in my direction as I entered. I felt stupid standing there like an object to be examined, but quickly realized that they were only trying to recognize an old buddy ... someone they may have served with.

Someone waved and gestured for me to enter all the way. I scanned all the faces again, as no one was wearing a nametag. As quickly as they turned toward the doorway—if they didn't recognize you—they turned back to whomever they were in conversation with and their eyes fell away. It was so long ago.... The men here had served in our company over a six-year period during the war. How would I recognize anyone? I headed for the bar. A tall guy standing near the corner of the room, wearing an old faded "boonie" hat, looked in my direction. I met his gaze. A huge smile erupted across his face.

"Hey Shorty, how the heck you been?"

There was no mistaking that voice, the New York accent. It was Gary Standish! I stood there in shock, gaping at him. The old boonie hat ... yelling to me that way. Suddenly I was nineteen years old again and looking at a teenage Gary Standish.

"Well, say something," he said as he approached.

"I'm just so glad to see you again; I'm just at a loss for words" I said. Tears were building in my eyes. I did not know such emotions could burst forth so easily from my soul. I wiped my eyes with the heel of my palm. Gary offered his hand. I took it in mine, and then forcefully pulled him close for an old buddy hug. I suddenly accepted that men can get sentimental at special times and that it is okay to hug one another. I noticed a little happy tear in Gary's eyes, also.

The moment was enough. It erased many of the ill feelings about Vietnam: I was with a man who knew me inside and out; a man who understood my fears and my joys. He was a man who had walked beside me during the toughest times and who would have given his life for me, as I would have for him. He was a man who trusted me to get him home again, just as I trusted him to do the same. We wiped our eyes, shook hands again, embraced again, and the magic moment passed. We fell to making small talk.

"Are there any others from our platoon here?" I asked, as I munched on a pretzel.

Gary handed me a beer, like it was a gift for old times sake. "I haven't seen anyone else, but I hear that most of the guys will be here. I can't wait.... When did you arrive?"

Assembly

I snapped the pop-top lid of the beer can and took a sip. "Just about two hours ago. I took a little nap first. ...went right from work to catch my flight and didn't sleep much the night before. I'm nervous, I guess."

"Maybe it'll be just you and me, Shorty—but that's okay. Hell, me and you.... We won the war all by ourselves, anyway." Gary slapped me on the back and let out a hearty laugh.

"Oh ... say.... I did meet Bob Tillis when I got in. Remember him? We rode the airport shuttle together. He's probably wandering around here somewhere."

"Great! Yeah, I remember Bob." Gary motioned me away from the bar and toward a table. "We have some catching up to do. Let's grab that empty table over there and reminisce a little. Hey Shorty, remember when you and I—"

It seemed as though no time had passed since Vietnam. We were young again and life was full of promises. We talked until long after midnight of old times and old friends. We talked of ambushes gone wrong and battles that we'd won. We relived the many patrols, recalled our commanders—good and bad—and the men who had died for their country. We laughed about things we once feared, and cried about the men who could not be with us. When our eyes would no longer stay open, we decided to call it a night, but agreed to meet for breakfast. The bed felt good and I felt good. I fell asleep with a smile on my face for the first time in many years.

VII

THE PARTY BEGINS

The phone jolted me awake. "Hey, get your butt up!" Gary bellowed into the phone. "Breakfast is waiting and so are some of the guys. I'll meet you by the restaurant entrance in twenty minutes."

I sat up and rubbed my eyes for a moment, contemplating whether I should try for a few more Z's or take a quick shower. Then I remembered something Gary had said: "Some of the guys!" I could only deduce he meant more of our old squad had shown up for the reunion. I jumped from the bed and headed for the shower. With a quick wash and shave—hoping not to cut my face too many times—I was dressed and at the elevator entrance in fifteen minutes. It seemed like it took forever, but when the elevator door opened, I instantly recognized the one person standing there. "L.T.!" I yelled.

Startled, he took a few steps backwards. "Shorty! How did you know it was me after all these years?" He grew a wide smile, letting his luggage fall to the floor.

"How could I forget those sun-soaked, California freckles," I joked and reached for his hand, but the closing elevator door wasn't waiting on my handshake. As it bumped my arm, it quickly sprang open again. Lieutenant Schmitter grabbed my hand in both of his and drew me inside the elevator, then hugged me warmly. I wasn't at all embarrassed; we had shared so much together. I wiped my eyes, punched a wall button and we plummeted toward the first floor. "I was going up, Shorty."

"Umm... Sorry, Sir."

Lieutenant Schmitter laughed and said, "How have you

been, Shorty? You look good ... haven't aged a bit."

"I'm doing okay, Sir—"

"Sir? What's this 'Sir' stuff? I gave that up a long time ago. Just call me Eric."

"Okay, Sir... er, Eric. Naw, that'll never do. You'll always be L.T. to me and the rest of the guys."

I slapped him on the back. He slapped me on the back. We arrived at the lobby; the elevator door opened and a group waiting to enter seemed amused at two grown men slapping each other on the back and grinning from ear to ear. Suddenly I knew why I had served in Vietnam; endured the heat, the bullets, the sleepless nights on ambush. It was for my comrades, my brothers-in-arms. They were all that was important to me at that time. They were the men I depended on and the men with whom I had entrusted my life, and, I trusted L.T. explicitly. I guess we could hug and slap each other on the back without explaining it to anyone. I asked L.T. if he had eaten breakfast.

"Why, no" he said.

"Well hurry and put your luggage in your room and I'll get us a table." He agreed and stepped back into the elevator. I giggled a sinister laugh as I knew more of the guys were waiting at the hotel restaurant for me. This will be a great surprise for our L.T.

Gary Standish was standing outside the restaurant with several other men. I recognized Roser, but the others didn't look familiar at first. "Well, it's about time," Gary blurted out.

At that, the others turned and looked in my direction. I knew each face but could not automatically place names with them. Nevertheless, I felt a mixture of emotions—somewhere between fear and joy; fear that I might never be able to recall them or that I might not have performed well in someone's estimation. The hesitation passed quickly and I moved toward them, glad to be in the company of such gallant men, and glad that I had come.

"Ya'all late, boy. I guess I'll have to put you on extra detail.

Maybe a little crap burning would fix ya," said the heaviest member of the bunch. He was pointing at me and grinning.

Who is this? I thought for a moment, then suddenly it hit me. His slight southern drawl gave him away. It was Sergeant Lowell Browning. ... Sarge. I'd have never recognized him if we had passed on the street. That slim person I knew back then was twice his size now, but his demeanor hadn't changed one bit. The authority in his voice was the same and I started looking around for the metal drum and diesel fuel. Sergeant Browning had that effect on people.

Another man joined in the verbal melee. He wore a shiny black, wide brimmed cowboy hat and I knew this guy was from the west. *Wyoming, maybe... Montana. That's it, Montana.* I dug for the name.

"And I'll call headquarters and cancel your R&R," he said. "Can you dig it?"

It was Don Farmhouser, our platoon radio operator, and he *was* from Montana. He hadn't changed much, just a little older. Like me, he had a little less hair on top. There was no chance to respond to him, as more men spoke up and memories flashed through my head at lightning speed. From around the corner walked a guy just a few inches taller than me. "Hey guys," he shouted as if it were a question. "What's all this... planning a patrol?"

We all recognized him at the same time. He'd stand out in any crowd. The same reddish blonde hair, the freckles across his nose, the "Lil' Rascal" attitude.... It was John Meddos and he looked like he'd just stepped out of a shower. He was youthful, physically fit, and had obviously taken care of himself through the years.

"John Meddos, you son of a gun," I said. "You look fit, but you haven't grown an inch. You're still second choice in a tunnel rat contest."

We all stood there shaking hands, hugging each other and telling quick little lies about how we hadn't changed a bit.

The Party Begins

I was thrilled beyond explanation. There we were: a half dozen former combat soldiers greeting each other as if no time had passed—as if we had just stepped out of the jungle from our final patrol. If these were flashbacks I was experiencing, I wanted more of them. Suddenly I felt like a teenager again, full of devilment. "Hey guys," I said. "I have an idea! Guess who I met on the elevator and is probably on his way down right now?"

They quieted and looked at me with blank faces, shrugging their shoulders. "L.T." I exclaimed. "Lieutenant Schmitter. I met him in the elevator. Let's hurry and get a table large enough for us all. We'll ask a waitress to escort him to our table. ... treat him with the 'reverence' we gave him in 'Nam. When he sees us we'll all stand up and call out, "Oh, great leader, welcome to our humble banquet, or something on that order."

"Yeah, you haven't changed a bit, Shorty," Gary laughed. "Let's do it."

The guys agreed that it was a great idea and we asked the waitress to seat us near the rear of the restaurant. We figured we'd really pull one on him if he had to walk the length of the restaurant with us bowing and hailing, "Oh Great Leader." We didn't give much thought as to how we might look to the rest of the restaurant patrons. They'd just have to understand that even middle-aged men can be somewhat silly at times. I was glad Linda had decided not to come.

Don Farmhouser caught the spirit. "Let's put our napkins over our heads when we start kidding him."

"What for?" Sergeant Browning asked.

"I don't know, just seems like a good idea," Don replied sheepishly.

We took a quick look around the table: there was unanimous agreement on the idea.

"Well, ya'all go ahead, but I ain't puttin' a napkin on my head," Sergeant Browning growled. Bowing is enough. I want to get my breakfast before we get thrown out."

The waitress entered from the waiting area looking our way. L.T. was a step behind her. We quickly placed our napkins over our heads, as if we were some royal court jesters, and stood at military attention. At the moment he saw our table of men, I loudly exclaimed, "All hail our leader and more eggs for his men."

We all automatically snapped a salute and burst out laughing. He and the waitress stopped dead in their tracks. She turned and headed for another table, asking them if they needed anything else. She glanced over her shoulder several times, perhaps wondering if she should have come to work that morning. The other patrons, however, laughed with us. They seemed to be in a holiday mood and accepted that there was something special about our group. They remained silent, watching us, waiting for the next act.

L.T. was speechless, his mouth agape. We motioned him to join us, and then removed our paper bonnets to reveal our identities. He stood by the table for a moment, studying us; trying to find a hint of recognition in our faces; trying to recall someone from the past. He collected himself, made eye contact with each man, and began to call our names, one by one:

"Sergeant Browning, Gary Standish, Roser, Don Farmhouser, John Meddos, Shorty Mendez," he said as if our names were branded into his memory. "I never forgot.... I'd know you guys anywhere, even with those ridiculous napkins on your head."

He took his seat and somehow I felt proud—proud to have served in combat with this man. The restaurant patrons burst into laughter and some even applauded. Our waitress inched her way toward our table.

"You are all now on a crap burning detail," L.T. said sternly.

We laughed even louder. The waitress finally made it to our table, standing back an extra foot, just in case. Her presence helped calm us.

"Are you 'Gentlemen' ready to order?"

The Party Begins

"Lighten up, Sugar," Gary said. "We don't bite, even if we are Vietnam veterans."

She broke into a smile. "Heard about you guys…"

Sitting there looking and listening to the guys made my heart race. As we relived little incidents; laughed at events that once made us cry; asked about men we had once known and the men who did not make it back; it made those days seem like only yesterday. Rowdy as we were, one person would talk while the others listened and ate. We wanted to hear the other man's voice and perhaps catch the spirit of his personality once again. The war stories were unimportant.

We took turns either poking fun at the changes our bodies took over the years, or relating some brainless thing we may have done in Vietnam. We had all done something stupid that we'd remember forever. It was easier than talking about the tragedies we had witnessed, and it helped to forge our newborn brotherhood.

I spoke up: "L.T., remember that time a Viet Cong … a 'VC', walked up and squatted to do his … er, morning business … just on the other side of the tree where you were squatting?"

"I'm eating," Sergeant Browning said.

"Sorry, Sarge," I said with fake humility.

Roser piped in. "Yeah, I remember that. You didn't hear him until he passed gas so loud we all looked your way. The expression on your face was worth a million bucks."

I was now especially glad Linda hadn't come. Our waitress had disappeared. Patrons were departing en masse, paying their checks at the table, not waiting for their change.

Sergeant Browning closed his eyes as Gary picked up the story: "Oh, yeah, that was so funny. Especially when you both looked around the tree at the same time, saw each other and ran. Just remembering you two running in different directions, falling down with your pants around your legs is worth this whole reunion."

We roared with laughter, remembering the incident,

everyone except L.T. Even Sergeant Browning managed a slight smile. John Meddos stood and tracked down the waitress. "Another pot of coffee please," he said. "I think we're going to be here a while."

"We're out of coffee," she said.

L.T. agreed that his chance meeting with the lone enemy was one of his most memorable moments in life, but also a story he didn't tell his children. "I have an image I must uphold," he said. Then he laughed even louder than we did.

We finished breakfast and lined up at the counter to pay our checks. Our waitress was reading the classified ads in the morning newspaper, perhaps looking for another place of employment. Suddenly she laid the paper down and approached us. "Welcome home, guys," she said timidly. "I'll make sure there is plenty of coffee tomorrow."

Never a good judge of character, I almost wept.

We departed individually; some of the guys needed to unpack and call home to let their families know they made it to the reunion safely.

The reunion schedule listed a meeting at 1:00 p.m. We all agreed to convene again for a quick lunch, and then we'd listen in on the meeting. Reunions and their protocols were new to some of us and we didn't want to miss anything. I was eager to learn more about our reunion and to see if any others from our unit had shown up.

I wandered around the hotel checking out the gift shops for souvenirs to take home. In one shop, a tall gentleman approached me. He had his hand out as he approached and wore a friendly smile.

"Hi Shorty," he said, as if he had known me all his life. "I'm Bill Swift, the reunion chairman. I watched your little breakfast scene. I have to tell you, I enjoyed watching you guys ... glad you came."

Bill explained that as host, he had done most of the calling and locating of our veterans. I realized that he was the man

The Party Begins

who I had heard about; the man who had dedicated himself to finding all of us and bringing us together again. I was impressed and humbled in his presence.

"Thanks for finding me," I said. The call from Stuart was just what I needed."

"I wish they could all be here, " he said. "Is this your very first reunion? ...never got together with anyone before?"

"Yes, this is my first contact with Vietnam vets," I said. "That breakfast gathering was very special to me, even though we clowned around a lot. I'm very happy that I came and we're all looking forward to your meeting."

Bill was a talker, but very sincere in his offer to assist me and anyone else with information that might help us enjoy the reunion. "We have a great banquet planned for tomorrow," he said. "If someone from your group would like to offer a few words—maybe some highlights from your year in 'Nam—the earlier men would enjoy hearing it. Don't be shy."

"I'm sure someone would be willing," I said. "I recall that our guys are not the best public speakers, but they can sure tell a story. ... maybe too good. I guess the best man to speak for us would be our Lieutenant Schmitter." Realizing that I had just volunteered our lieutenant to take the stage at the banquet, I asked Bill for his silence as to how he acquired L.T.'s name. He grinned, understanding that L.T. was being volunteered without his knowledge. He slapped me on the arm and we both laughed.

I asked Bill if he had read the article in the previous day's newspaper about the Vietnamese General and his good will political mission. "He's in this area," I said.

"No kidding ... a Vietnamese General? I hadn't heard about that," he said.

I quickly responded, "He's supposed to speak at a political luncheon somewhere here in Nashville. I never met any Vietnamese except their soldiers and we weren't too friendly with each other. Maybe we could invite him to speak here at our banquet tomorrow evening?"

"Now that would liven up the party!" Bill replied. "Can you just imagine one VC General and a couple of hundred American infantrymen in one room!"

Although we both laughed, clearly he was intrigued by the idea. I dropped the thought. It was probably something too much to expect and perhaps too much for our guys to accept. Our experiences in Vietnam were not all amusing. In fact, most of them were tragic. "No love lost..." as they say.

Bill jabbed me lightly in the stomach. "I have to get things ready for the meeting. I'll see you there."

I finished shopping and decided to go to the hotel's register desk. I asked the clerk if any names on my list had checked in. He looked at the names and checked them against his registry for Charlie Company. "They've all seem to have checked in except one person." He said.

"Who's that?"

"A gentleman named Simmons. ...Stuart Simmons ... from Iowa."

"Ole' Hayseed!" I shouted and clapped my hands.

"Whom?" the clerk asked.

"Oh, never mind ... just had a flashback."

"A what?"

"Skip it, Son. Just please give my buddy my room number when he gets in."

"Yes, Sir. I'll tell Mr. Hayseed that you left explicit instructions— "

"Yeah, okay..." Maybe we were a misfit class of people that could no longer communicate with the general populace.

"Thanks for the help," I said and headed for the elevator. It was packed with reunion members: veterans, and also some ladies who I assumed were their wives or girlfriends. A few children were stuffed amongst the crowd, hugging their parent's legs, obviously in awe of "big" people. I knew the feeling.

The Party Begins

Next time, I'll bring Linda ... just won't take her to breakfast....

As the elevator sped toward the upper floors, I could hear the quiet murmur of an old rhyme coming from the rear. "Row, row, row, your boat, gently down the stream..." It was Gary.

"Merrily, merrily, merrily, merrily ... life is but a dream," I spontaneously replied. The crowd broke out into song and the children came out from their mother's skirts. In those few seconds, we instantly became a family. We were men and women from different backgrounds, living in different parts of the country, each with their own diverse lives, but we had been brought together by a common experience.

"God is good," someone said.

Men from different years of service in Vietnam got on and off at different floors. At some stops, we held the elevator to allow someone to finish their introduction or their tale. It was interesting to listen to men who had served a tour of duty in Vietnam, at a time before or after I was there. It seemed we all had stories, all of which held a ring of familiarity to them. As the old saying went: "the same story, just a different place in time." I never tired of listening to them.

There is a certain amount of pride in having honorably served one's country, especially during the fourteen-year period of the Vietnam War. Some former soldiers, and many Vietnam veterans, believe that their experiences were the most tumultuous, the most dangerous and that they fought the most awesome battles of the war. It is a natural thing to believe that your combat service was vitally important, lest the entire contribution may have been for nothing. I can therefore understand their braggadocio—their swank—and singing their own praises.

Sometimes it is too much to swallow, however, and I was irked by the vet who commented: "We were there before you, so we cleared the way!"

One man said: "All the big battles were happening when

I was there in '66."

Gary Standish retorted by saying, "Does that mean the fifty thousand or so who died after you were there was by natural causes?"

Patriotism is a powerful force among men. I was sure a fight would ensue as the boisterous guy turned red when he realized the remark he made was taken to heart by Gary. He turned quickly and headed to a safer area of the hotel meeting room. I had never seen Gary so serious. "Don't mind him," I said.

"I just don't like the idea that a fellow vet would try to diminish our time and efforts in Vietnam. I might just put a can of "Brooklyn whup-ass" on him later." Gary was back to normal.

The period of time, whether it was a full one-year tour, or if a man had been wounded and left early, would always be a very sensitive area of discussion, but one we knew we had to keep in perspective. We cannot always measure the other man's suffering from his remarks.

When I later mentioned the scene to Bill Swift, he commented: "Don't mind old 'Fatso.' He's healing."

I never concerned myself again with absurd comments from a show off. "They're healing," I would repeat Bill's wise introspective.

The tense moment had passed and we decided it was time to go to our rooms and ready ourselves for the night's events. At his afternoon meeting, Bill advertised our banquet, scheduled for the next evening, as a potentially "unique" event. "Very special," he said

I busied myself making sure my dress pants and pressed shirt hadn't become wrinkled, packed away in the suitcase. I hung them up to let any creases relax. I picked up the telephone and dialed my home number. The phone rang busy at home. I guess that meant that someone was at home and all was well. I decided to call back later.

The Party Begins

There was a knock on my door. "Come on, open up" a man yelled. I knew it was John Meddos trying to pull one over on me, so I played along.

"Who's there?" I yelled back.

"Police, open up!"

"I can't. I have several wild and naked women in here and they don't want their husbands to find out! Go away ... come back tomorrow."

"Ok, ok, so we aren't the police. But we're hungry and ready to head to town for a big 'water buffalo' steak. You coming?"

I opened the door and stared into John's face. Behind him were most of the other guys. I grinned as John still had to sneak a peek over my shoulder; just to be sure there weren't any women in my room.

"Where they at?" John asked.

"Jumped out the window ... yes, I'm coming."

VIII

THE VC GENERAL

Plenty of drinks loosened our tongues as we as we enjoyed our dinner. "Hey," Gary Standish said to the group. "Do you remember the day we humped for maybe eight or ten clicks and it was about a hundred degrees in the shade? We ended up so exhausted.... L.T. had us set up an early ambush ... about noon."

"Oh, yeah. I kind of remember that one," L.T. said. "It was hot. Some guy— "

"Let me tell the story, L.T." Gary laughed. Gee, it's one of the few incidents I remember real well."

"Aw, go ahead, tell your story Standish," Sergeant Browning said. "But remember, get it right... we were all witnesses.

Gary continued: "Some guys pulled guard duty while others took turns napping. Later in the day, and all of a sudden, one of our 'Kit Carson' scouts let out a yell and began rolling all over the ground. We didn't know whether to laugh or if he was having a seizure or something— "

I interrupted: "I remember that. I thought he was having a religious experience or a premonition of his death. ...ever hear of that?"

"It's my story, Shorty."

"Sorry, man."

Gary chugged his mug of cold beer and slammed it on the table. He wiped the suds from his mouth and leaned forward. We were all ears, although we knew the story.

"Well, turns out while he was napping, a giant lizard had

crawled up onto his stomach for a warm nap, like we were doing. He never felt it. When he awoke and opened his eyes, he was face to face with this reptile. His reaction was to grab the lizard's head and wrestle with it—"

"I believe it was a large lizard, not a giant lizard, Standish," Sergeant Browning said.

"Okay, okay.... A big lizard.... Well, do you guys remember that about an hour later we had our first taste of stewed lizard? I can still taste it." Gary was elated: He had managed to finish his story.

"That calls for another round," Don Farmhouser said. Get the taste of lizard out of our mouths... gunpowder, too. Flag down that pretty waitress!"

We all laughed, acknowledging the incident and agreeing that the lizard tasted unusually good and we would drink to the memory of the taste. The evening wore on and we shared other tales from Vietnam. One by one, each member of the group told his story. Sometimes it wasn't quite the way I remembered it, but they were good stories, nonetheless. We drank and made numerous toasts: some to each other ... some to our friends who didn't make it home. It was a good time ... with good friends. I slept well that night.

The telephone rang: "Hello."

"Wake up call, Mr. Mendez."

"Uh, thanks" I said.

I slowly rolled off the bed and headed for the bathroom.

Oh, my head. ...now where are those aspirin? I should have known better than to drink with those guys. They always were able to hold more than me. After a lengthy shower I headed to the hotel restaurant. Our same pretty waitress approached me with a smile.

"How are you, today, Sir! Isn't it just a beautiful glorious day? Where are your friends?"

I raised my head from my hands. "Please bring me a large cup of coffee. Black. Make it a pot."

"Okee, dokee, soldier! One large, black, cup-o-joe, comin' up!"

What in the world has gotten into this female? Yesterday she dodged us like we had lice; today she wants to bust my eardrums with her style of customer relations.

I gazed around the restaurant and noticed several other reunion guests sitting with their heads in hands, a cup of steaming coffee below their half-awake face. Seeing them made me feel a little better, especially as our bouncy waitress heaped the same sunny weather report on them. She took an order or two from them and skipped back into the kitchen.

"Oh, God," Farmhouser moaned and put his head back in his hands.

Bill, the reunion host, walked into the restaurant and took a seat next to me. He looked around the restaurant, smiled a knowing smile, and shook his head. "I'm glad I was too busy last night to go out with all you guys," he said looking towards me.

I forced my eyelids open, smiled, and feigned non-association with the guys at the other table. "Yeah ... poor souls had a little too much to drink. Don't know why they do it."

"It's Okay, Shorty. They deserve to blow off steam after what they experienced. You, too." Bill grew serious. "Hey guess what? I thought about your idea of having that Vietnamese General speak at the banquet tonight."

I was stunned. I wasn't feeling like any jokes or clever stunts that might involve me, especially so early in the morning and nursing a nasty hangover. *Wish Linda was here.... I'd be having orange juice.*

"I know you'll be pleased," Bill continued. "I called the mayor's office and got information on where the general was staying. They gave me his hotel and number. I called and left a message to have him call me back if he had any interest in speaking at our reunion."

"You did! ...didn't mention me, did you? Ah, here comes the coffee..."

"Yes, would you believe that he called back yesterday evening and accepted our invitation? He'll be here tonight at the banquet. I guess we'll have another opinion about the war ... from their side. Might arouse a lot of different memories."

"Wanda The Waitress" screeched to a halt at the edge of the table, pouring my coffee and sticking the cup right under my nose. The hot steamy brew smelled good. "Enjoy!" she shouted. "Get you anything, Mr. Swift. We have a special—"

Bill took her hand. "No thanks, Jillian... just checking my chickens this morning. Tell your mother I said hello."

I sat up straight. "Jillian ... you know her? You know her mother?"

"Yes, she's a member of our church and so is her mother. They've been living hand-to-mouth since her father was killed in an automobile accident recently. I managed to get her a job here when I arranged the reunion. Yesterday was her first day."

"And we were her first customers, right?"

"Yes, and she told me about how you guys carried on ... frightened her to death. She's heard a lot of nonsense about Vietnam veterans. She thought you might set a fire or set off some explosives."

What changed her attitude? She's all smiles today."

"One of your guys wrote her a note before leaving. ...apologized for the group and said he understood her fear. He asked her to try to understand us. ...left a big, big tip."

"Aw.... That's nice. I thought she was a schizo. I can see that we Vietnam veterans might stir up some strange feelings about us ... the way we acted."

Bill leaned across the table, looking me dead in the eye. "Speaking of feelings, I'm sure our general is going to stir some up. ...guys might even want to talk with him, express their feelings. But, the war is over and we're all grown men."

I leaned across the table, too; but I didn't stretch as far as Bill. "Express their feelings? You'd better hope someone doesn't try to tear his head off. I agree most of us can forgive and forget, but I'm sure some of the guys will be ready to start the war all over again. You didn't mention me?"

"As a matter of fact, I did. I asked that your name be included in the banquet program as the personal host for General Toi. The Chamber of Commerce was delighted to have a forum for him."

"You did what!" I exclaimed, almost spilling my coffee.

"I understand he's not controversial ... won't try to justify their views. He's on a goodwill trip, trying to establish trade ties and all that. Don't worry, you'll both be a big hit. ...want to introduce him?"

I slumped back into my chair wondering if there was an afternoon flight back to Tampa. *Roser, Gary, Sergeant Browning, what will they think? These guys hate the Viet Cong.... They'll hate me, too.*

Bill stood up, came around the table and put his big arm across my shoulders. "It'll be all right, Shorty. Remember, I Said we are all healing, and we heal in different ways. This will just be a part of it ... be brave. Our guys need to hear this former enemy ... get them to thinking ... calm the rage. It isn't good to hate." Bill moved in front of me and I looked up at him, surrendering to his wisdom.

"Okay, we're healing. I think I'm about all healed, however. I'm sure the general's talk will be no problem with the guys. I'll begin by spreading the word early so most everybody will be prepared for his visit. I'll start over there."

I shook Bill's hand and headed to the other table where my gang sat. They were still breathing coffee and saying very little. Gary played with his eggs. I clapped my hands and rubbed them together, over and over, trying to build a little enthusiasm (and conviction) for what I was about to tell them.

"Hey guys, guess what!"

"What...?" John Meddos brought his head up. "Oh, it's you, Shorty. How's your head this morning?"

"We'll see you tonight," Bill shouted as he left the

The VC General

restaurant, grinning.

"Guess what, what?" Gary asked, his head still in his coffee. "Speak your piece."

I decided to be diplomatic, spring it on them slowly. Searching for the words, I remember Bill's admonishment: "Be brave."

"We have a guest speaker tonight and you'll never guess who it is ... General Toi."

"You mean like General Electric, we have a General Toy? What's he do, make G.I. Joe's?" Gary asked.

"Tell us about it, Shorty," Sergeant Browning said between bites of sausage. He was the only one at the table who was not hung over. "Who's this general? Where's he from?"

"Well ... ah ... he's from Southeast Asia." Several heads came up from their coffee.

"Where in Southeast Asia?" Doc Barult asked.

"North ... Southeast Asia."

"Doesn't make sense, Shorty," L.T. said. "Where's he from...?"

"Vietnam."

"South Vietnam ...our side?" Gary asked.

"North."

Four heads bolted upright. Sergeant Browning put down his fork and picked up a knife. He chewed slowly on his sausage.

L.T. turned and looked at me. "You mean South Vietnam, don't you?" he asked.

I was committed: "North Vietnam," I said clearly.

"North Vietnam!" Farmhouser shrieked. "You mean from when we were fighting the war? We have a communist guest speaker?"

"Who's damn dumb stupid idea was that?" John Meddos asked. "We shot his kind."

"Well.... I guess ... me, I think. I tipped Bill Swift off that the guy was in the area. ...read it in the paper." *They're healing ... be brave.*

I sucked my body up to my full height. "He's not carrying grenades or an RPG or anything. He's on a goodwill tour, trying to represent his government, I guess. What's the harm?"

"I'm carrying ammo," Gary said. "I'll shoot—"

"Cool it men, " Sergeant Browning ordered. "Let's hear what the man has to say. It might clear up some things. Like our Tunnel Rat says, what's the harm?"

"Yeah, well, okay," Gary said. "But I'm bringing a pistol, just in case."

Sergeant Browning, as always, had the desired effect on his platoon members. Out of respect for him or the wisdom of his words, they all agreed to attend the banquet and listen with open minds to our former foe.

"What time does "your buddy" take the stage, Farmhouser growled. Then he broke out into a grin. "Just kidding little buddy ... we know you meant well."

"Thanks guys. ...looking forward to it. I'm going to my room for a nap. Didn't get enough rest. Say, tip that waitress real good; it's part of healing..." I quickly left the room. I could hear John Meddos saying, "part of what...?"

There, I did it. But I think I'm going to need plenty of aspirin before this night is over.

IX

OUR FORMER ENEMY

Checking myself in the mirror, I thought that I hadn't aged that much. I had a few wrinkles here and there ... a little gray, but not bad. I remembered my eighty-three-year old grandmother saying the same thing as she headed out the door for the horse racetrack. Her advice was that it wasn't how old you looked, just how young at heart you felt. "Just don't look in the mirror after forty," she cautioned.

I sucked in my belly to fasten the waistband of my dress pants. Tying and retying my necktie several times, I realized that I was nervous, thinking about the bombshell that was about to be dropped on our reunion group. I shouldn't have brought it up.

What will the guys from the earlier groups think, and those who came later? They don't know me; they don't know what a sweet and wonderful person I am. Was Sergeant Browning studying my neck when he picked up that knife? Be brave....

The phone rang. It was Linda. "I sure hope the banquet is a peaceful one tonight," I said.

"Hey, husband of mine. Thought I'd give you a call. Having fun?"

Oh, yeah, Honey ... loads of fun. Our banquet is only a few minutes away. I'm a chicken.... I mean I ordered chicken."

"Steve, are you all right? I hear something strange in your voice. What did you say about hoping it was a peaceful banquet?"

"I said 'peachy' banquet. You know, peachful."

"You did not."

"Maybe not ... don't know what I said. I was only thinking out loud."

"Why are you a chicken? You said you were a chicken."

"How's the weather down there?"

"Why are you a chicken?"

As all good and loving wives do, she would not let go. I told her about the newspaper article on the North Vietnamese general and how I had inadvertently gotten him invited to our reunion. I confessed that my best buddies, who I had not seen or heard from in years, might very well send me home in a body bag if they didn't like what the general had to say.

"I'm going to sit way in back," I said.

"Steven. First, from what you said, it doesn't sound as if you invited him to the reunion, Mr. Swift did. Second, he may very well be an excellent speaker and add something to your occasion. We are not still enemies with Germany or Japan. Third, no one will know it was you that got the ball rolling. Mr. Swift has to deal with that."

"I'm on the program ... listed as the host for the general."

"I see.... Well, have fun, Honey, and call me tomorrow. I'm going over to church right now and meet with my prayer group. We're praying for world peace. I'll include you. Be brave..." With that, she hung up. I straightened my tie again.

The banquet hall was full and noisy as I entered and looked around. Everyone seemed in a joyous mood. The open bar was already busy and the line never emptied.

"Hey, Shorty. Over here!" It was Gary Standish, John Meddos, Larry Cummings, Stuart Simmons, Doc Barult and most of my old platoon. Many more men had arrived since our breakfast meeting on the first day. Stuart had come in during the night and he hugged me mightily. He held me at arms length, appraising me. Then released me and held my arms

"Good to see you, Shorty. You haven't aged a bit ... look the same. Aren't you glad you came!"

"Oh, yeah. Hayseed. Real glad I came. Good to see you, also."

"What's the matter, buddy? Still hung over? I heard about that party."

"I'm fine, I guess. My head is just full of thoughts, remembering the way it was."

"Well, we'll fix that tonight. Put away the past, live for the present, I always say. C'mon, let's sit."

They had commandeered a large round table for our platoon. I joined them with handshakes and smiles all around, as if this was our first meeting. Everyone was in a celebration mood. Their chatter and gawking at the beautiful place settings and banquet hall adornments seemed to occupy them for the moment. No one mentioned the guest speaker. I realized that my apprehension was without basis, and surely, the general would be gracious. I might even get a pat on the back for having thought of it. I decided to forget it, let the chips fall where they may.

I selected a seat where I could view the dais. I wanted to see my former adversary up close. I had to admit that Bill Swift had done an excellent job in arranging this reunion and preparing the banquet. Against the back wall, behind the stage, a huge American flag had been draped. Its brilliant colors of red, white and blue sent chills up my spine. A banner had been posted above the flag. In bold letters it read: **WELCOME HOME, CHARLIE COMPANY, 3RD BATTALION, 22ND INFANTRY. REGULARS BY GOD!**

Although most of us had been civilians for many years, we were still proud of our American heritage, the unit we fought with, and the men we fought beside.

A small table with clean, starched, white linen sat next to the stage. It had a place setting of fine china, wine and water glasses and an enlisted soldiers cap. Among some of the items of military paraphernalia, a small sign announced that this was the "Missing Man Table"—set as a symbol that our fallen soldiers would never be forgotten. I thought of the men killed in action and was sad that they could not be with us. We would memorialize them later with a reading of their names. A mist filled my eyes.

A disk Jockey was setting up in the corner, ready to play the tunes of the 60s and 70s, I had been told. An after-dinner dance was planned as well as a charity raffle. The banquet hall was immense, and I scanned the tables for familiar faces, finding only a few. My guys were all assembled here with me, and that was enough. I turned my chair around and focused on our table... my guys. Every one of them was intently reading the program.

In unison, they peered over the program, glaring at me. In addition, in harmony again, they laid their programs down and glared some more. For a moment, I wanted to run and almost did. Then I realized that the entire scene was too choreographed to be a spontaneous reading of that program. They had set me up. I slapped the table and gave a loud hoot. "You guys gotta' be kidding me!"

At that, the entire group broke into loud laughter. Indeed, they had orchestrated the incident, knowing how sensitive I was to the issue. It was their way of saying: "That's all right, Shorty. We are still your buddies."

"The hell with that general," Doc Barult said. When do we eat?"

They all started some small talk and joked of the previous evenings debauchery and their morning hangovers. John Meddos ordered a couple pitchers of beer and glasses for our table. "Let's do it again," he said.

Sergeant Browning and L.T. came into the banquet room. They spotted our table as we were all at attention with a salute to L.T. Their eyes rolled and they turned and walked away as if not to recognize us. Farmhouser caught up with them and ushered them to our table. We all had a good laugh over it and poured our Sarge and L.T. a beer.

L.T. raised his glass and proposed a toast: "Gentlemen, and the rest of the guys at this table. I would like to toast my appreciation to those men who served under my command; some unwillingly and some without a choice. Really guys, I'll always remember you men as friends and hope we meet again often. 'Toast!'" We held up our glass and toasted a drink to each other.

"My, you've gotten sentimental in your old age, L.T." Simmons said. I thought you hated me way back then."

"No, Stuart, I felt the same then... just couldn't show it. I'm glad to have the chance to say how much I appreciated all of you. You got me back home safely."

We didn't need any more toasts; we just raised a glass and shot knowing looks to each other. That was good enough. The dinner and service was excellent compared to other formal banquets I had attended. My chicken breast was superbly prepared and was delicious.

"What is this chicken?" I asked. "It's great. Linda might like the recipe, but it probably has some strange sounding French name."

"They call it 'Southern Fried,' Shorty," Sergeant Browning drawled. "You're in Tennessee."

"Well, it's darn sure better than C-rations!" I announced. Suddenly, in the midst of our laughter a quiet hush fell over the table. We noticed a well-dressed oriental man sitting at a table near the front of the banquet hall. "That must be him. General Toi," I said.

"How can you be sure... ever seen him?" Larry Cummings asked.

"His picture was in the newspaper. That's him."

"He doesn't look so mean," Gary said. "I can take him ... he pisses me off."

"Looks to be about sixty," Sergeant Browning observed. "Right age considering he's a general and all."

"Gentlemen, let's stop gawking," L.T. said. We agreed to

let it drop... let him have his say."

As the dinner tables were being cleared and we settled into small conversation, Bill Swift approached the podium and grabbed the corners. He cleared his throat several times, and finally got the attention of the audience. "Gentlemen, soldiers of Charlie Company... again let me welcome you all to this reunion. I'm overwhelmed at the great number of men who have made it to this wonderful gathering of Vietnam veterans. As Saint Paul said: 'Lord, it is good for us to be here.' All of the men in our locating committee did a wonderful job in finding a large number of you Charlie Company Regulars. Our membership has doubled this past year. I believe we should give a round of applause for our locator group!"

Obediently, we roared our approval for the men who had spent the last year combing the records to find us and bring us together. Bill, our Master of Ceremonies, went on and on with reunion information, recognizing those who deserved acknowledgment and appreciation. He thanked everyone involved, mentioned some highlights about to come during the year, and informed us of the evenings remaining events. Most of our guys talked in quiet conversations, with only a slight ear toward what Bill was actually saying. I was on the edge of my chair, listening to everything... waiting on that magic moment.

Bill looked up, paused for a long time, cleared his throat and said: "Now. Ladies and gentlemen, we have a special treat for you..."

Here it comes....

"Only through divine providence are we assembled here tonight... so many men cannot be with us. And by that same fate, we have a unique opportunity to hear about those circumstances in Vietnam from a man who faced you on the other side of the rifle. Yes, I'm speaking of one of our former adversaries, a Viet Cong soldier. He will speak to you in a moment."

Bill stopped, took a long swallow from a glass of water,

and looked over at me. A slight murmur rumbled throughout the crowd.

"Our two countries are at peace now," Bill continued. "Regardless of our ideologies, in spite of our past; we are speaking to one another, building trade alliances, and many of our men have visited Vietnam as tourists in recent years. Our men come back with stories of how beautiful the women are, and how elegant some of the hotels are. Why, I understand that Nui Ba Den, the mountain site of many of your battles is now an amusement park. Yes, things have changed... and in my opinion, we must change. The pain of Vietnam is too great to carry to our graves."

The silence in the room was stifling. No one said a word, coughed, or rustled in their chair. Bill drank from the glass again. He took a deep breath, looked across the sea of stony faces and continued.

"Divine intervention...? I don't know... but just yesterday, it was brought to my attention by someone who shall remain nameless ... that a former combat commander of a Viet Cong unit was traveling the United States on a goodwill tour. It so happened that he was right here in Nashville; a guest of our local Chamber of Commerce. One thing led to another and he is here with us tonight."

Nameless.... Nameless! Hot damn!

I reached for a program. My name was not mentioned.

Oh, thank you, Bill!

I wasn't listening to his introduction any longer, but I did hear the words: "...introduce to you General Nyen Toi."

The reunion hall became a low murmur of quick conversation, rising to a peak as the general walked from his table to the podium. He was stately, with squared shoulders, and gracefully glided across the floor. He deftly bounded up the steps to the stage and smiled at the audience—his former enemies.

A few patrons in the crowd gave out low volume cat calls

of "VC," "VC." Someone from the rear shouted, "VC … you number ten Charlie."

Still others applauded. I thumped the table, clapped my hands, and yelled, "Right on!"

Bill Swift graciously shook the general's hand. As General Toi stood at the podium and looked over his audience, a silence overtook the men in the room. His gaze, as it went from one side of the room to the other, seemed to captivate them. I appraised our guest from Vietnam as a very courageous man, and a man who had a strong enough character to face his old foes. He was surely a leader of the highest caliber. In excellent English, with only a slight hint of oriental dialect, he began:

"Gentlemen, I am honored to have been invited to speak to the brave men of Company C. Regular soldiers, I am told you are called. That word has meaning in my armed forces, also. You are not 'holiday help' as some might say." He smiled as a slight chuckle emitted from the audience.

"He damn near got a laugh on that one," Gary said.

The speaker continued: "Your history as a formidable fighting force preceded you before Vietnam. If we speculate, we might even say I could have met some of you before, on the field of battle, hence my knowledge of your gallantry. I have the best respect for you."

A few in the hall applauded his comments; others shook their heads knowingly to one another. The general had calmed their fears by his clever use of praise and compliments. I was warming up to him.

"Yeah, we were good... damn good," John Meddos said.

"And we didn't lose no war," Sergeant Browning blurted.

"Shh, listen," L.T. reminded us.

"I came to the United States to meet with your political leaders to help mend relations between our two countries," General Toi said. "As a soldier... like you, I know the hard feelings held for so many years: those feeling of hate, fear, and misunderstanding. The sorrow long held for fallen comrades…

memories of fierce battles won and lost. I am here to let you know; I and my fellow soldiers of the new Vietnam ask that we both put these memories to our past. We must look for a new and better future for both our countries. Let us reach forth a hand from our country to yours and from yours to ours. I ask of you now, let it be over! Let all our brave soldiers finally feel a peace with themselves and each other!"

General Toi seemed to have finished, but quickly remembered to express his gratitude to everyone before he left the stage. "I thank you for inviting me here, Mr. Shorty, wherever you are. I am happy that you read the newspapers and tell Mr. Swift about me. You have all been a very kind group of soldiers and I thank you for listening to me. If you come to my country some day, maybe I can treat you well like you have done me. Thank you!"

No one seemed to look my way when he said "Shorty" so I didn't duck under the table. My guys had already settled it in their minds. The general didn't leave the stage, but instead stood there, smiling; staring out over the sea of faces. I wondered if someone would do something to embarrass us all. Slowly a few men at a time stood up and applauded. Soon, most of all the men, including our table, stood and applauded. I even noticed some men wiping their eyes.

"Aw, he's okay, I guess," Gary said. "I won't mess with him."

Others agreed, but Doc Barult was still sitting. He had his arms folded across his chest in defiance. He did not applaud.

"What's up, Doc?" I asked with just a touch of "Disney" humor. He had enjoyed the play on words in Vietnam.

He replied, "I can't applaud anyone who may have done the things I had to try and patch up over there. I was a Medic, damn it! ...trying to save lives. You should know ... you were there the same as me and saw what some of those gooks did to our guys."

I hadn't thought of Doc too much over the years. He was a

brave man and he never refused to make a house call, even in the heat of battle. He obviously felt very deeply about his experiences in Vietnam. It must have been tough for him to have to patch up wounded men; the very men with whom he ate and slept with every day. To have to look into the eyes of the severely wounded, as their lifeblood flowed away, and hold them as they died. It was a nightmare for the medics. Even I might feel such an awful hate deep inside; perhaps a hate that could never be healed. It might be too much to expect that Doc could look through the eyes of his enemy and see and feel the camaraderie—the new partnership the general had suggested.

I put my hand on Doc's shoulder to let him know I understood. We all sat back down as the general walked away from the podium and returned to his table. Bill took the microphone again. "The general will be our guest for the rest of the evening and he has asked that any and all feel free to ask him questions. I'd like to thank you for your courtesy to the general. So, let's all have a great time. The bar will be open all night. Thank you."

The house stood again and applauded, acknowledging Bill's outstanding efforts on our behalf. The reunion was first-class and everyone felt it.

"L.T., what do you think of the General?" Roser asked.

We all looked at our lieutenant with a questioning grin and raised eyebrows. "I'm thinking about it," L.T. said. "Offhand, I'd say his remarks were appropriate. A lot of what he said is true. Our countries do need to put the past aside, for a better political future. But it is essentially a communist country. Every nickel spent by G.I. tourists and others over there goes to support a socialist society. The people are still enslaved. I can't help it; I'll always have bitter feelings about Vietnam."

We shook our heads in agreement, each of us thinking the same thing: Maybe we could forgive, but we would never forget. Doc grunted to acknowledge L.T.'s remarks and the comments of the others.

"Excuse me gentlemen." We turned to acknowledge the person who interrupted us, demanding our attention. Our eyes went wide and our mouths fell open as we recognized General Toi, standing there at our table.

"Yo, what it is, Sir," Meddos said. "Can we help you?"

"I am sorry to interrupt your conversation, gentlemen. I presumed it would be easier if I approached first. I understand the hesitation one must feel when a former enemy of war is suddenly put face to face with his adversaries so unexpectedly."

We shook our heads—agreeing—feeling a little less tense at his presence. A long period of silence followed the general's eloquent comments. Finally, Gary Standish spoke up.

"Were you a General during the war, uh... conflict?"

"No, I was a political leader then. Your rank would have me as equal to a colonel," he responded. His smile was perpetual and he disarmed most of us easily. All except Doc Barult.

"When exactly did you enter the service in Vietnam?" Meddos asked.

"My family has always been partisans with the People's Army in South Vietnam. I suppose you could say that I was always a soldier. We have faced many wars over the centuries. During my youth we were all trained for ... expected to become soldiers. My mother said that I was measured for a uniform one hour after my birth."

We caught the humor and also recognized the vast suffering of the Vietnamese people. The questions began to come easier from us and a chair was offered to the general. He readily joined us. Then Sergeant Browning asked a question, which when answered, silenced us. "Where or what area did you control?"

Unhesitating, the general answered. "My area as a political provincial leader was an area west of Ho Chi Minh City. You will recall it as the city of Saigon during the war... er, 'conflict' as the American politicos like to say. The city was renamed to Ho Chi Minh City when the North and South were united as one country again. I controlled the western most area in the province of Tay Ninh."

"No shit," Doc said dryly.

We sat there staring at the general. The silence at our table was obvious to the crowd even through the loud laughter and fun that was going on throughout the banquet hall. We had served our entire tours of duty in Tay Ninh province. It was a vicious battle ground. The coincidence unnerved us all. Bob Tillis decided to step in. Bob was always a diplomat of sorts among the platoon members, settling arguments over C-rations, foot powder, beer, and used up Playboy magazines—to mention a few of the things we argued about.

"Hey guys? How about another round of drinks for everyone?" he offered.

Doc saw his chance to get away from the table. He jumped up and replied, "I'll get the drinks." He headed off to the bar. We slowly came out of our self-imposed state of shock and silence. I guess we all were thinking the same question, but found ourselves hesitant or even afraid to ask. The general sat there coolly, neither offended nor concerned with our reaction.

Larry Cunnings, who was never one for tact, blurted out, "Hey, you were in the same place as us!" At that very moment, Doc returned with the refreshments. He barely set the tray on the table before we all simultaneously reached for a drink. It didn't matter what was in it; we all needed it. I was hoping Cunnings comment would go unheard.

"Did you say you were in the same area as a soldier?" the General asked Cunnings.

"If you said Tay Ninh, General ... that's where we were at ... all of us," Cunnings replied. "Maybe we know you...."

We sat silent again, this time waiting for a response from the General. We gave Cunnings a look—a look that made him understand that he had said something we didn't want to hear. He grinned and covered his mouth in a gesture of false shame.

"How interesting, how very interesting," General Toi remarked. "Who would have believed this chance meeting;

former adversaries of separate countries connected by world history and the need for commerce? To be reacquainted by a lucky chance meeting more than three decades later is opium for the soul; a destiny in our lives. Surely, this was meant to be? You agree, no?"

"I don't know about opium, General, but it certainly is an odd coincidence," I said.

"Ah, you must be the Mr. Shorty that your wonderful Bill told me about. I hadn't noticed you before. I wanted to meet you and thank you personally for bringing us together. I understand you went into our tunnels … a tunnel mouse they called you."

"Rat, I was a tunnel rat … not a damn mouse."

"Oh, forgive me," General Toi replied with a smile. "The nuances of your language escapes me. You have a large animal, a moose I believe. Therefore, I assumed the mouse was the larger of your rodents. Nevertheless, you are a brave young man. We had many miles of tunnels … all of them occupied."

"Well, thanks, General. Would you like a drink? Help yourself, there's plenty here."

Doc glared at me.

"Tell me gentlemen; it is no longer a military secret. What was your unit?" the General asked.

L.T. replied that we were a part of the 25th Infantry Division. "We were called "The Regulars.""

"Ah, I know this unit," General Toi replied. "My men fought this unit on many occasions. Your soldiers were a most formidable foe. I salute you and your men Lieutenant." He reached for a glass and held it up in a toast to our unit and the "remarkable challenge they presented to me at one time. Your valor will never be forgotten! Bravo!"

We spontaneously joined him in the toast. *Heck, he's giving us more credit than our own countrymen did after we got back.*

"Please excuse me gentlemen," General Toi said. "But my time is limited here tonight. Please accept my gratitude and great pleasure of meeting with you. I am most honored to have spent time with men who made history together with me and the men who served with me."

Lost in a moment of thought the General hesitated, and then continued speaking. "Let me propose a question before I leave. If my country is willing and provides the means, would you, Lieutenant… and your men, accept an invitation to attend a similar reunion in my country?"

L.T. looked dumbfounded as he searched the faces of his former command. He was never one to comment without thinking it out beforehand. "What do you guys think?" he finally said

"Why not," I said. Lot's of Vietnam veterans have been going back and they say the places we fought are hardly recognizable. It's safe now." The others nodded or spoke in agreement with me.

"Bill said the women were beautiful," Stuart Simmons said. "I wouldn't mind checking that out."

"I always wondered what it would be like to go back for a visit," Gary added.

"Me, too!" Roser piped in.

We began talking all at once. L.T. quieted us down as the General motioned for silence.

"My consulate will be in touch with your Lieutenant Schmitter. If all is agreed to by my country, I will help with the arrangements. Thank you so much for your hospitality. This chance meeting—your reunion—has been a most long sought event in my career. I am getting older and the ravages of war … military service ... have taken their toll. You men have made my life nearly complete. I will do everything in my power to help the next reunion be your most memorable one.
I must leave now. Let me stop and say good-bye to your fine host, Mr. Billswift. Thank you, and until later… good-bye."

We sat quietly around the table in thoughts of our own. "Hey Sarge, do you really think he'll try and have a reunion in

'Nam?'" Cunnings asked.

"If he does I doubt if he can have his country pay to fly us all over there... and that's if we wanted to go! I think he was just being polite since he was invited to ours."

"Could you imagine us all over there again? I'm not sure if I really would want to see that place again," Roser said.

"Ah! Let's just forget about him," L.T. said. Have another round of drinks. We should enjoy ourselves before we have to leave tomorrow. I'll get the next round."

"I wonder if they still have crap burning details over there?" Gary laughed. "If they do, Shorty's the first one on it 'cause he started all this mess. We laughed together as we had all had that detail at one time or another, except of course for Sergeant Browning and L.T. The crap burning detail was a job you'd never, ever forget. The smell still permeated my nostrils and my brain, and it did the same to everyone. I suppose that's why we mentioned it so often.

We finished the evening, having shared with each other fond memories and tall stories of our gallant deeds. We still held that closeness we had when we were together in Vietnam. It was a nice warm feeling, something down deep that tells you that even with our own little faults each man of our unit respected and trusted each other. Somehow, we all managed to end up in our own rooms, to sleep away a night's worth of wonderful camaraderie, not to mention the partying. I drifted off to sleep knowing that I too, was healing. I hoped the others felt as much peace as I did at that moment.

A brilliant sun burst through the window curtains and morning came much sooner than I wanted. My banging head reminded me that I just couldn't drink like I used to. I had some satisfaction when I went to the restaurant for my dose of hot, black coffee. Most of the guys were there, just as on the previous morning, with heads held in their cupped hands.

"Oh, my head's going to break open!" Gary Standish groaned. "Whose idea was those last rounds of drinks?"

"You guys are on my crap burning list," L.T. said. "My head feels like we drank a gallon of Tennessee whiskey.

"You did," I said

"And I don't even drink… anymore," Gary said.

Our waitress, Jillian, was as perky as ever, and she kept us supplied with hot coffee.

"Listen you guys," I said. "I have an early flight and need to pull out. I want to thank you all for being here. I don't know how to express my feelings about this weekend, so how about a handshake and I'll be on my way."

Everyone stood and gave each other handshakes and buddy hugs. We all promised to keep in touch and meet again at our next reunion. I left Jillian all of the folding money in my pocket. Not much, but I was feeling some kind of sentimental mushiness in my stomach and it wasn't the whiskey.

"Love you guys," I said, and departed for the airport.

X

SPECIAL INVITATION

*F*our years passed after that Tennessee reunion. Although Charlie Company held reunions every two years; I had missed a couple of them due to either business problems or the lack of time or money. Gary Standish, Stuart Simmons, and Larry Cunnings, along with several others of the platoon, kept in touch by letter or telephone. A newsletter from the Company C organization kept me up to date on the association and reunion happenings.

Gary had written recently reminding me of an upcoming reunion. It was to occur the following month in a city not too far from me. This year I was thoroughly prepared. I had hidden away a little money here and there over the years; enough to pay my expenses and even a few souvenirs.

I was mowing my yard when the mailman drove up. His usual stop and go procedure changed this day as he drove up into my driveway and stopped. A very huge man, I marveled at how nimbly he stepped from his mail car, waving a letter in the air. I could hear the air being sucked out of the shock absorbers.

"Mr. Mendez, good morning. I have a special delivery letter for you," he said.

"Not from the I.R.S., I hope."

"No, looks like it's from overseas. ...lot's of colorful stamps. I signed for it and he climbed back into his jeep to continue his route.

The elegant envelope had very unusual stamps and fancy cancellations marked all over the front. I knew it was important.

I wondered how the mailman could read the address. *Maybe it's from one of those contests and I've won a million dollars.* I decided to wait a few minutes before opening it. I didn't want to drop dead of a heart attack on my front lawn. I went in the house to get a cold drink. "Who's the letter from?" Linda asked.

"Ed McMahon," I said as I poured myself a cold glass of iced tea.

"Let me see, Stephen." I handed her the envelope. She was better at handling serious matters than I was. "It appears to be from an embassy in Vietnam. Who do you know there, Mr. Big Shot? Is there something you haven't told me?"

"No.... No. I can't think of anyone," I replied. "Maybe someone who knows me took a tour there or something?"

"Well, open it," Linda said. I carefully opened the envelope and pulled out a neatly folded letter typed on what appeared to be high quality paper. The embossed letterhead in red and gold boasted the national flag of Vietnam. A slight rage welled up within me, and then just as quickly, subsided. The message was short and to the point:

"The government of Vietnam cordially requests the pleasure of Mr. Steven Mendez's company at a combined reunion of the members of the Third Platoon, Company C, 3rd Battalion, 22nd Infantry, 25th Infantry Division, U.S. Army, and the members of the People's Command Unit 468 of the new Republic of Vietnam.

All arrangements are compliments of the People's Government of Vietnam. Please complete the enclosed confirmation card and promptly reply. All details and information of personal concern will be delivered to Mr. Mendez upon acceptance of this invitation."

    Sincerely,
    General Nyen Toi

I sat down in the first available chair. I had completely forgotten that day in Tennessee when General Toi first offered to reunite us in Vietnam. Linda took the letter from my hand.

Special Invitation

As she finished reading the invitation she said, "Are you going to go? You've always talked of wanting to make a return visit some day. Now you can go for free!"

I drank the rest of my cold tea. "I'm really not sure," I said. "The invitation is from the General from Vietnam who spoke at the last reunion I attended. He said he would try to arrange a reunion in his country, but we all just figured he was being a politician. I never thought he was serious and I haven't even considered it since then."

"Why don't you call your friend in New York and see if he received an invitation? If your whole platoon is going, you might not want to miss out."

"Good idea. That's why I married you."

The phone rang several times before Gary Standish answered. "Guess who?" I joked.

"Hey Shorty, are you calling about that invitation to 'Nam?"

"Yeah, did you receive one, too?"

"Sure did ... I already mailed back my reply."

"...you going?" I asked.

"You bet I am!" Gary sounded excited and gleeful.

"Hey, it's a free trip to Vietnam for a week and all expenses paid for. I couldn't pass it up. You're gonna come, aren't you?" Gary asked.

"I don't know just yet, I received the invite only a few minutes ago. Knowing that you're going helps me make my decision though. I tell you what... I'll call the other guys and see if they all got invitations, too. If they did, and most of them are going, then I'll consider it. I'll call you back..."

"Sure, I'll be waiting for your answer," Gary said.

I polled everyone I knew, calling them at any hour of the day or evening. It seemed like they were all waiting by the phone, expecting others to call. Almost everyone had just finished talking to someone else. All of them had received a special delivery invitation like mine and they too, were trying to decide. Most agreed that they would like to travel to this oddly proposed gathering of Vietnam veterans. Knowing we'd go as a group, as a platoon again, made it easier to decide. It appeared that the Vietnam reunion was on! I called Gary and relayed the information that most of us were ready to head back to Vietnam again. "You got point man," I said.

"You got crap burning," he laughed, and then grew serious. "I know we joke a lot, Shorty, but have you given any thought to the fact that we are supposed to meet with General Toi's men; unit 468?"

"No, I haven't thought about that, but I guess we won't be normal tourists. What the heck, we might have a better time than the average sightseer... see more of our old stomping grounds."

Gary and I agreed that it would surely be a safe trip. The war had been over for decades. We agreed to make the best of it and have as much fun as we could.

I pondered over my decision, uncertain if I made the right choice. Linda suggested that I was feeling the fear of the unknown. My thoughts of seeing the guys again, however, overcame my reluctance to go. Besides, I was going for free! Then I laughed as I remembered that we went free the first time. I wrote out an acceptance letter to General Toi and mailed it to him.

XI

RETURN TO VIETNAM

*M*y **plane landed in Los Angeles to change flights. I had** a two-hour layover; enough time to grab something to read. Looking over the rack of magazines just inside a concession, I felt that sensation you get when you know someone is staring at you. I picked out a Newsweek and slowly turned around to see if someone really was watching me. There, about twenty feet away, stood a group of five or six men staring at me over the edge of their newspapers and magazines.

Now who could this be? I thought. The setting reminded me of one of those old Bob Hope and Bing Crosby spy movies. I opened my magazine and lifted it to my eyes to spy back over the pages at them. My mimicking them caused them to break up with laughter. I should have known that somewhere along the route to Vietnam, I'd run into some of my old buddies.

I greeted Gary, Larry Cunnings, L.T. and the others. It looked like most of the platoon was going back. After some small talk, we headed for the nearest airport bar for a drink. "What about getting something to eat before the flight?" I asked.

"That's the idea," Gary said. "We'll drink dinner here!"

I succumbed to the suggestion. I would survive long enough and surely have a meal on the long flight to Vietnam.

As we drank our "pork chops and potatoes" I asked, "Are you guys ready for this trip?"

"Sure," John Meddos said. "I packed all kinds of stuff. I even brought a poncho in case it rains."

"No, No," I replied. "I meant, did anyone have second thoughts? I know I'm still a little hesitant… don't know what

I'll feel once we're there. I guess I'm confused because I don't feel bitter towards anyone—except maybe a few politicians."

"We all feel like we left something behind," L.T. Said "I know I feel that way, but haven't decided exactly what it is I'm looking to find. I'll just have to prove to myself that I really did make a difference while I was there… that my service meant something." Most of the guys nodded in agreement with Lieutenant Schmitter. As a leader, there were few better than him and I was glad he was going with us.

"By the way, Meddos, what 'all kinds of stuff' did you pack?" Sergeant Browning asked.

"A full carton of candy bars, a few pocket knives… just a few things to hand out to the kids like we did back then. I always did enjoy giving out food stuff to the kids when we had a chance."

Sarge looked up and rolled his eyes jokingly, then said, "I hope customs doesn't give us any hassles over that stuff when we arrive. I'd hate to end up in one of their prisons."

Stuart Simmons chimed in. "I've been reading some magazine articles written by guys who went back. I understand you pay your way through customs. Always keep and extra ten or twenty dollar bill in your shoe and you'll never be bothered."

"So it's a capitalist society after all," Doc Barult remarked.

The public address system blared, announcing our flight. We killed our drinks and headed to the gate. We were flying "Air Vietnam" and the Vietnamese attendant asked me if I had my passport, which I handed him. Confused by the English words, he matched up my picture by holding it beside my face for several seconds. The process was slow.

"Would you like all our passports together?" I asked.

"How many in your party, G.I.?" the attendant asked.

"Let's see now… twelve all together," I said. I was stunned that he used the word, G.I. How the heck could he tell after all these years?

He smiled. "Yes, let me have them all. We check photos while we fly. Somebody give them to Vietnamese customs agents when you arrive. There will be less trouble that way."

"Trouble?" Don Farmhouser remarked. "There will be trouble if I don't get my passport back."

John Meddos echoed his concern, then asked: "He called you, G.I., didn't he? You guys think he knows we're a group of Vietnam veterans?"

Sergeant Browning spoke up. "Hell, just about every American going to Vietnam is a veteran of the war. G.I. is a universal word... fact is, it's a compliment."

I felt no apprehension about returning to Vietnam. I was with the best men, the best friends a man could have on this earth. As I remembered General Toi, he seemed to be an affable man. What could happen to us?

We were seated as a group. The attendants treated us with courtesy and efficiency. We settled in for a long flight, looking forward to a refueling stop in Hawaii. *I guess there is no turning back now.*

I looked around at our little group. It reminded me of a newsreel I saw on TV showing POWs returning from North Vietnam. They all had solemn, blank, and apprehensive looks on their faces. I presumed we were all hiding feelings similar to those returning prisoners of war; some private unknown emotion that most veterans keep for themselves. It was just the reality that we were really on our way again, back to a country that we never wanted to see in the first place, and a country that we were darn sure glad to be out of when our tours were over.

As the plane leveled and we relaxed a little more, we began reading our magazines. Some were talking while a few leaned their chairs back to relax or nap. The flight to Hawaii was uneventful. We refueled there and lifted off again after a thirty-minute stretch break. Gary and I commiserated over the fact that we didn't get to see any "Hula" girls. The flight was half over now, and actually, I was happy that we weren't wasting any time. The pilot came on over the intercom and said, "Ladies and Gentlemen, off to the right side of the plane you can see the lights of the Philippine Islands."

I remembered the first time I had seen these islands. We had stopped to refuel in the Philippines when I first flew to Vietnam in 1969. I thought that we were landing in Vietnam and couldn't understand why everyone was so calm. When I asked the stewardess (they called them that before political correctness took over our society) where we were, she told me, "the Philippine Islands." I sighed with relief having been given a few hours reprieve before facing the battlefields of Vietnam. I related this story to Gary who was sitting next to me. He remembered that same flight and added that he also became a little more worried as the flight approached Vietnam.

"Too bad I didn't know you then," he said.

I teased him how we all acted so tough and brave while debarking the plane in Vietnam.

"Yeah, I didn't get to know you until that first night when we went out on wire guard. You were my first friend. Our being in Vietnam together gave us a sense of brotherhood ... something to help each other when we really were afraid."

The flight attendant then announced, "Please fasten your seatbelts, we'll be landing in Vietnam, Ho Chi Minh City, in approximately fifteen minutes. Thank you for flying with us and have a good visit." From that moment on, until we felt the wheels touch down, we were silent. My thoughts raced through many different events of my tour, confusing me as to how I should react to being in Vietnam again. The stillness of the group indicated they shared the same feelings. Similar feelings had raced through my mind before landing thirty-years before. This trip, I'd just have to feel out... play it one day at a time. *But, wasn't that how my first tour was—one day at a time?*

I thought back to the time my army experience began.

XII

THE MAKING OF A TUNNEL RAT

I recalled many events before entering the army in the summer of 1969. Some of them left lasting impressions; others were misunderstandings about the war. I was just finishing my senior year of high school and wasn't paying much attention to anything except fast cars and pretty girls. Little by little, I became aware of antiwar demonstrations erupting in my hometown. It angered me. My older brother had been away in Vietnam, for a long time. He was a role model for me and I wanted to follow in his footsteps. I thought that, I too, was ready to do my part for the war effort.

The students at our local university had been demonstrating against the war and they were getting a lot of attention. My high school friends and I would stand on the fringes of these demonstrations, hoping to see squad cars of police arriving and watching them throw tear gas into the crowd. One whiff of whatever they were using and the demonstrators would bolt and run in every direction. We would stand back and laugh, watching the students coughing, crying, and running from the irritating chemical. It was better than a three-ring circus. We weren't active participants; we barely had much knowledge about current events and didn't really understand the motivation behind the demonstrations. Nor did we care very much. I assumed it was somebody else's war and it would all be over before I graduated.

At some point in these regular demonstrations, a more radical group decided to use a large bomb to blow up a university building. There were injuries and a lot of destruction.

The violence brought the issue to a higher level and I no longer thought of it as a game. I lost all respect for the students and quit going to watch them.

Maybe it was my upbringing, my age, or just personal pride, but I felt the Vietnam War was a just cause. I believed that we were trying to free innocent people from the yoke of communist oppression. Why else would our country send young men to fight a war? I knew that I would eventually join the Army: it was my patriotic duty. My brother had done three consecutive tours and I missed him. I had some naïve view that if I joined the war effort, we could fight together, side by side. I'm sure that if he had been home sooner, he would have stopped me from volunteering for the draft lottery.

I remember the day I came home and found my mother very upset with me. She showed me a letter from the Department of The Army saying that my request to be drafted had been honored and that I should report for a physical examination. As she sat there on the edge of the sofa, crying and waving the letter at me, I felt a little guilty about what I had done. I just wanted to see my brother again and share in his "adventurous" lifestyle. "Stephen, I just can't understand why you would want to do such a thing," my mother wailed.

It was a good question.

My brother finished his tour of duty and came home just a few months before I went for my induction physical. For some reason he thought I was the dumbest kid alive for signing up. He said I would surely go to Vietnam, and that I didn't want to go there. During those last few months, he would constantly tell me how behind every bush there was a horrible poisonous snake and behind every rice paddy berm there lay a hidden enemy, waiting to shoot me. He had me thoroughly brainwashed and scared. I made mental notes on his every word. I would be prepared if I saw bushes or rice paddy berms.

I reported for my physical in Milwaukee, Wisconsin. We spent most of the first day taking aptitude tests. In the afternoon,

The Making of a Tunnel Rat

we took more tests. I must have done well, because later they told me I would be in the Infantry. "Only the finest men are selected for the Infantry; the Queen of Battle," one recruiter announced.

My chest swelled.

We finished the exams late in the day and the government gave us lodging for the night. It was my first experience being away from home, staying in a motel all on my own. "This army is all right!" I said to my three roommates.

The next morning we returned to take a physical exam. It was like a cattle call. We stood in line and inch-by-inch we shuffled up to a doctor who would order us to stick out our tongues. Then he'd tell us to turn sideways for an inspection of our ears. "Look straight ahead," he growled.

It was my first experience with a grouchy physician. I assumed he didn't like being stateside and would rather have been in Vietnam where he could hone his medical skills. Or, maybe he was just tired of looking at tongues and eardrums. I was glad I hadn't decided to become a doctor.

Comments and opinions abounded when we were told to line up in rows, drop our pants, bend over, and "spread 'em!" The bad-tempered tongue and ear doctor walked behind us, stopping on occasion to examine more closely, the physical characteristics of our rumps. "You got some real good assholes in this bunch," he said to the top sergeant overseeing us. They both broke into fits of laughter. They took our height and weight. When they weighed me, all 92 pounds, they laughed again.

The top sergeant recommended I eat more: "Put some lead in your ass!" was how he explained it.

When they measured my height, all 4-foot, 10 ½ inches, the doctor said, "You'll never pass the physical restrictions." It seemed that the army had a weight and height limit.

"You must be at least five feet tall and weigh a minimum of 102 pounds," the sergeant said.

I really feared that my size would actually prevent me from

fighting for my country. I wanted to be like my big brother. I couldn't imagine that they would put me through two days of testing and an expensive physical examination for someone to say, "you're too small." I had grown up hearing that every day of my life. I just couldn't let my pride be kicked again. I knew I could be as big as anyone else!

At the completion of the physicals, all the statistics were given to the head medical officer for evaluation. He was the final word on acceptance or rejection. Eventually, I heard my name called. I entered an office to see an older military officer sitting behind a gray metal desk, peering through bifocals at a folder. I noticed his look of concern as he examined my records. Finally, he looked up at me and grinned. Then he sat back, took off his glasses and laughed. "I actually thought someone was playing a joke on me with these size and weight figures, but I see now you are this small. Well, it's your lucky day. I'll have to reject you because you don't measure up. How do you feel now… glad that you won't have to go to Vietnam?"

"Lousy, Sir" I responded. "I didn't volunteer and go through all this testing to hear 'You're too small' again. I can fight and be a soldier like anyone else!"

I stood there as the officer looked me over. After a long wait he said, "You may not know what you are saying... what you are asking for. Do you really think you can do this ... be a soldier?"

I told him I could handle anything a big guy could handle, maybe better.

"I admire your spunk, Stephen Mendez. I wish everyone I examined had your attitude." He looked through some papers, studied one of them for a moment and after a long pause, said, "I think I have just the position for you, Son. You would be perfect for it. Congratulations, you're in the army now. We'll accept you."

I watched as he scratched off something on the reports of my physical. I guess I felt relieved; my pride was back in place,

The Making of a Tunnel Rat

but I didn't ask him what the position was. The officer stood and shook my hand. "Good luck, you'll need it!"

I took the remark lightly until later in my training. Only then did I understand the full meaning of his "good luck" warning. As soon as I exited the office, I opened the folder to see what the doctor had written. He had scratched out the areas showing my true height and weight and had rewritten the qualifying minimums of 5'0" and 102 lbs. Now I knew the army was the place for me. I had grown an inch and a half and had gained ten pounds in just a few hours.

Later that day we were ushered into a room with a podium and the U.S. flag. An officer in a full dress uniform, bedecked with ribbons and medals, stood before us. He said that anyone who was opposed to being sworn into the armed forces should take a step forward. No one did. The officer told us to raise our right hands and repeat the oath of office as he read it. I remember saying that I'd defend my country … against all enemies … foreign and domestic. I gazed at the flag. It was an awesome moment! When we were finished, he congratulated us and said that we were now members of an elite group of Americans: "soldiers in the armed forces of the United States!"

He departed and the Top Sergeant took over: "Ok, you sorry-ass bags of horse crap, line your maggot-eaten asses up in single file in the hallway. Move it!"

We scurried like rats running from a bonfire. I said to the fellow ahead of me, "And I thought the tongue doctor was grouchy, what's got into this guy?

"I don't know," he replied. "But he can't talk to me like that. When I get home I'm going to tell my mother and she'll call … tell him a thing or two."

I decided not to tell my mother.

I figured we'd be led off to some other area. I was surprised to see this rather large, mean looking, white haired man, dressed in a spectacular uniform with a million stripes and lots of ribbons on it. Someone said, "That's the Marine Sergeant.

He's going to pick a few good men for the Marine Corps!"

My sweat glands immediately activated. I wanted to go Army as my brother had. The Marine sergeant slowly walked down the line of men. (I mean boys).

"Pathetic, does your mommy know you're here?" he asked rhetorically. "I need real men. Who has the balls… who thinks he can cut it as a Marine? Step forward if you're a man. Leave the ladies standing there for the U.S. Army!"

Two guys took the daring step. The Sergeant quickly stepped in front of them with his face a scant one-inch away from the shaking volunteers. He stared a long cold stare into their eyes, then said: "Do you wet the bed, Fagot?"

One young guy with a very squeaky voice replied, "No, Sir."

"Then I guess you might be a Marine someday, Fagot. Get in my line!"

I presumed that once you became a Marine, you also become a fagot.

"Okay! I need six more," he shouted. He'd walked down the line and if he found a prospect he'd just stare at him then say, "You're gonna be a Marine, Fagot. Get in my line!" I actually thought one guy was going to faint from his violent shaking when the Marine sergeant stepped before him.

The Sergeant stepped in front of me, but just stared over my head. I didn't move a fraction of an inch. After a long pause, he finally spoke out in a loud voice: "Is someone supposed to be standing in this space?"

Soon, he looked down and laughed aloud. "I guess someone lost their little brother. Are you lost, little boy?" he said.

I looked up at him a little angry and spoke before thinking: "No, and I can't be a Marine because I'm not a fagot."

Several guys openly laughed, but the quick, hard stare from the Sergeant quieted them immediately.

The Sergeant looked at me with the look of death, his face all red and small beads of sweat appearing on his forehead.

The Making of a Tunnel Rat

"No you ain't gonna be a Marine 'cause we don't take babies!"

As he stepped away, I quietly replied, "just fagots." I spent the next four hours cleaning toilets, polishing fixtures, and moping floors, but at least I was in the army.

After a sorrowful family parting, I was off to Ft. Campbell, Kentucky for basic training. I spent the next eight weeks there. Surprisingly, I really did enjoy all the physical exercise and marching. I had no problems concerning my height, except for a lot of ribbing I received from the drill sergeants. I felt that all the yelling wasn't necessary, but learned to keep my opinions to myself. I had my share of K.P. (kitchen police) duty and most of all, I hated peeling potatoes. They still peeled them with a paring knife by hand. It was very tedious and time consuming.

Next, I was off to Ft. Polk, Louisiana, for advanced infantry training. Ft. Polk is a very old and very isolated training camp. Our barracks were built for WW II and they looked like it. There were still watering troughs for horses and mules at the front of each building. The training areas were solid jungle and surrounded by swamp. It was hot, humid, dusty, and a hellhole of a place. It was a far cry from Kentucky. We lived in the "North Fort" area, cut off from the main post.

In retrospect, I'd say the soldiers who trained at Ft. Polk, gave a good account of themselves in Vietnam because of having learned their skills there. The tropical conditions, especially the vegetation, were very similar to what they found in Vietnam. We learned the fighting tactics of a jungle warrior, and we learned to shoot straight—if we were unlucky enough to go to war. Our drill sergeants seemed to love to do long road marches every few days. I hated the long marches because they would have us line up in formations with the tallest men in front, graduating to the smallest man at the rear. Those tall guys sure took long strides—so long in fact, I inevitably had to shuffle-run just to keep up. At first I thought I'd never survive this particular training episode, but I eventually found the other guys respected my determination, which helped me endure the long marches, uh ... runs! Graduation was a great day. We felt proud, physically fit, and ready for anything. They gave us a weekend pass and said orders for assignment would be posted on the following Monday. Most of us received a promotion to "Private First Class." Wow! A pay raise! Now we made $148 a month. I thought I was rich.

All the guys discussed the probability of jobs and the locations of their new assignments. Most just figured we would surely go to Vietnam. Secretly I think we all hoped for a European assignment. On Monday, after breakfast, we all waited in our barracks, sitting on the edge of our footlockers or beds, anticipating the posting of orders. Finally, one man spoke out: "Here comes the Senior Drill Instructor and the other sergeants. He's carrying some papers... bet it's the orders."

Someone yelled, "Attention!" We all stood as the Drill Instructor entered the barracks and posted our new assignment orders on the bulletin board. He walked to the center of the barracks and announced: "I want you guys to know that you have been the hardest working trainees I've ever had. I'd be proud to serve with any of you. Good luck! Check your orders and then pack your personal belongings for a two-week leave prior to your new assignment. That is all!"

I figured the speech was one he gave each training class on their last day, but I did appreciate the sentiment. I was the last to get to see my orders posted on the board. Since the papers were about two feet above my head, I waited until the crowd cleared, and then craned my neck to see where I'd be going. In bold letters the orders announced my future:

SPECIAL ORDER NUMBER 4342:
Mendez, Steven J.   S.S.# 020-34-6789
Private First Class, E-3
Reporting Date: 28 October 1969
Duty Station: Republic of South Vietnam

Almost everyone had the same orders. A heavy silence fell over the barracks and we sensed the reality of it all deep in our souls. Until this decisive moment, Vietnam and war was still something we only played at in training or observed others actually doing on TV newscasts. We were really going.... We were really going to war!

The two weeks at home before departure to Vietnam would go by in a flash. I wished we would have more family time when we did get home. I thought of friends who were killed very early after their arrival in Vietnam. They only had two weeks to say good-bye. Forever....

To comfort ourselves, we decided to go to the P.X. and purchase some beer and snacks. We decided to have a good graduation and departure party. We had just begun our party when the Senior Drill Sergeant entered the barracks. He stood at the doorway and just looked around the barracks as if he were searching for someone in particular. We were sure it was K.P. duty instead of a two weeks leave, but he just stood there and looked around. He made no mention of our party and the forbidden alcohol.

His eyes eventually fell on me and he said, "Mendez ... new orders. Come and get 'em." Then he said, "Isn't anyone going to offer me a drink?" Everyone let loose and the party began. I wandered over to the posting board to read the new orders:

SPECIAL ORDER NUMBER 4343:
Mendez, Steven J.   S.S.# 020-34-6789
Private First Class, E-3
Duty Station: Fort Polk, LA
Purpose: Special T.R. Training.
Duration: One (1) week

The orders then went on to say that I had to report immediately. I wouldn't be getting my two week leave. I asked the Drill Sergeant what "Special Training, T.R." meant.

He said he had no idea. "Never heard of it before."

I was thoroughly confused. The only special training I ever heard of was for kids in school who couldn't learn. *Oh, no! Where did I screw up? I passed all the tests. I even ran a million miles.*

I was distraught, imagining that I had done something wrong and had to be retrained. What special training did I need? I had to report the very next morning. My home leave would be delayed and maybe even cancelled. I slept very little that night. The next morning, as instructed, I reported to a building with a sign attached: "Special Ops and Weapons Training."

I entered to see a clerk at his desk. He looked up as I entered. I handed him my orders and asked if I was in the right place. He looked over my paperwork very carefully, and then he looked me over very carefully. "I can see why they picked you."

"Why me," I asked. "And for what?"

He said, "I really can't say. The Sergeant in charge of training will be here in a moment and he'll explain. Have a seat."

That's just great, I thought. No one knows anything and no one says anything. Hurry up and wait.... You're in the army now.

A Sergeant entered the office slamming the door as if it were the natural thing to do. The clerk handed him my orders. The Sergeant turned and reached to shake my hand, making me feel at ease. "I'm Master Sergeant Miller," he said. "Come on in my office and I'll explain your selection for this special type of training."

I was at a loss. Why me, and what special training? It was like reporting to your school principal for an unknown reason. We entered his office and sat down.

"Do you have any idea about this training?" Sergeant Miller asked.

The Making of a Tunnel Rat

I told him I had graduated from basic training only yesterday and reported to him today. I asked, "no one seems to know what this training is about."

"Well," he said. "Do you know, or have you ever heard the term, 'Tunnel Rat'?"

"No, I haven't."

"Then allow me to explain. For many years during recent history, especially the history of Asian wars and during WWII in the Pacific ... even Korea, our enemy used tunnels and caves as a means to hide and store men and equipment. In Vietnam, the enemy has spent many years constructing tunnel complexes to do the same. They have created a vast network of tunnels in Vietnam, along with natural caves and bunkers."

"When one of the tunnels or caves are located, we do not have trained personnel to enter and search these complexes. We've been depending on volunteers to enter and locate either the enemy or stored items within them. We call these volunteers, 'Tunnel Rats.' They are a necessary element in an infantry unit over there and it is a highly dangerous job... without prior training. That's why we decided to start a training program for tunnel rats. Unfortunately, we aren't getting qualified volunteers. In fact, there never were any *qualified* tunnel rats before this school.

"You said, dangerous, Sergeant?"

"Yes, but every job in Vietnam is dangerous. With your unique size, you'd be selected to go down into tunnels anyway. At least here, you'd be trained and have a greater chance of surviving."

"Makes sense..."

Sergeant miller, a graying, but physically fit man, continued with his explanation. He seemed like a caring individual, soft spoken, and proud of the fact that this tunnel rat school was under his command.

"I've only got two of you as trainees right now, but this school will grow. It was something I had in mind ... saw as necessary after my last tour in Vietnam. Just got it approved."

His description of how the school had come about and what it would do for me was interesting, but I pretty well had the picture. I could see me down in some sewer with other rats, picking through the enemy's garbage, hoping not to get shot.

"At this training facility, we've constructed a simulated tunnel system to train special people to do this type of job. We'll train you—the first man to attend—in all facets of entering, searching, capturing prisoners, and destruction of tunnels, caves, and bunkers. Your special abilities upon completion of the training will give you a distinctive position in your assigned unit. Any questions?"

"No, Sergeant."

"Good soldier…!

"Thanks, Sergeant."

Sergeant Miller smiled. "Say, you don't mind if I call you Shorty? It seems so natural."

"That's okay, Sarge.... It doesn't offend me. But you asked if I had any questions and I said no. Actually, I have a million of them, but I really don't know what to expect, so I guess I don't have any questions right now." My mind was a blank at all he had explained. I was somewhat confused, unable to grasp the big picture.

"Okay, get settled into the barracks," the sergeant said. "At 0600 hours tomorrow morning, meet me at the training room next to the barracks. And, welcome to 'Special Training.'"

The clerk directed me to the barracks and familiarized me with the area facilities. I put my clothes away and rolled out the sheets and blanket on one of the bunks. I had just finished making my bed when a man about my age entered the barracks.

He looked surprised to see me and quickly asked, "Are you here for the T.R. School?"

I said, "Yes, are you going also?"

"Not only no, but hell no!" he said. "I'm here for something else. I've been waiting for two days for some midget to arrive.

The Making of a Tunnel Rat

Could that be you?"

He smiled and held out his hand. "I'm Mike Boykin ... Pittsburgh."

"Midget?" I asked; a little defensive.

"The guys just said a really short guy was picked out to be the first army trained tunnel rat. Some doctor spotted him up in Milwaukee."

I asked, "Aren't you going to be a tunnel rat?"

"Like I told you before, no way. I'm here to learn demolitions, that's all. I guess they'll teach us both at the same time."

"Maybe I'll search and you can blow them up, Ha!"

We both had a laugh over it and then went to the mess hall for lunch. We spent the afternoon getting to know each other and read some training books the clerk left on our beds. They were very boring, as most army training manuals are. I was soon fast asleep, having learned very little from my reading.

XIII

TUNNEL RAT EXAM

*W*e spent the first few days learning a history of how different countries used tunnels and caves as a military advantage. We learned how simple and how complicated they could be, and especially how dangerous they were in Vietnam.

After reporting for duty the next morning, the sergeant took us by jeep to an area he called the training grounds. There, a tunnel complex had been constructed. It was a set of simple ditches approximately three feet wide and four feet deep. One ran about twenty feet long and another about ten feet long. It had one side open for visual instruction. The top was covered with plywood with dirt covering the plywood. There were also two bunkers. They were typical sand bag bunkers. A good-looking grass hut had been constructed to represent a Vietnamese village.

We spent the morning hours with Sergeant Miller as he taught us the proper methods of search, safety, and demolition theory. He told us to go ahead and search the first tunnel the best way we could manage.

We really had no idea where to start or how, so we approached the most easily seen opening. I told my partner, Mike, to secure the area outside and I would check the hole. He stood by representing that the area was safe from enemy intruders. I tried to concentrate and remember the things I had been taught. I reached the edge of the opening and reached in to feel the inside edges.

BAM! An explosive device immediately went off. I nearly crapped my pants from the surprise.

Tunnel Rat Exam

"You're all dead! That's how easy you can die if you don't know how to start," Sergeant Miller exclaimed.

I just sat in the dirt, a little shaken by the surprise and the realization of how sudden death might occur for me as a tunnel rat.

"You learned a valuable lesson, Shorty. Let's go sit in the shade and I'll teach you about surviving as a tunnel rat."

The training became a series of scenarios of searching simple looking, but very deadly, little holes in the ground. Over and over again, the tunnels and bunkers would be set with hidden, tricky, booby traps. But with each search, I began to learn a strategy of the tunnels and how to suspect every inch of dirt. My training days were passing quickly.

On one test, I had to do the entire tunnel system at night. I could only use items I found at the complex to use as instruments for searching. I could not use my flashlight on this search. How could I find a trip wire, an electrical contact? I learned to trust and do what the instructor asked—and use my natural senses.

Mike said, "I have the area secure, go ahead and search." I trusted Mike as his training in demolition and securing zones for demolition had taught him well.

I started my nighttime search at the hooch (grass hut). A thorough outside search on hands and knees discovered nothing. I continued with a low search of the entrance and still found nothing. I crawled inside, continuing my exploration. I found a plastic picnic knife and I kept it for a tool. A plastic tool doesn't conduct electricity when it meets an electrical arming device. I exited the hooch exhausted, but determined. I told Mike the hooch was ready for demolition. I assisted as he planted a simulated TNT block of explosives to blow the grass hut. I decided to search the bunker next, as it would take less time than a tunnel would.

The bunker was also empty of explosives or persons. We had been searching for three hours with nothing to show for it.

I hadn't learned yet that finding nothing was the prize because no one would be injured or have to take the chance of injury.

Mike and I took a break for water and some sandwiches we had brought along. We discussed the next search and in what manner I would approach the long tunnel, if I found it. To start the search again, Mike gave me the "secured area" signal.

I crawled toward a large rock, which had previously given me a bearing to the tunnel opening. I crawled and searched for twenty minutes and just couldn't find the tunnel opening. I knew it was near that rock. But, no matter how long I searched; I just couldn't find an opening.

Growing impatient, Mike asked: "What's going on. What's the hold up?"

I told him I had to change my strategy. I was really concerned that I had missed something. I told Mike to be extra alert. He said he would double secure the area.

I used the light of the moon to keep my bearings as I mentally marked area boundaries. I searched by going to knee-walk movements forward, carefully using my fingers to test the ground surface. With every inch of ground I touched, my palms lightly pressed for a weakening in the ground's resistance. Sweat was rolling into my eyes. I would try to wipe the sweat away with my hand, only to mix perspiration and dirt into my eyes. I learned to wipe with my shirtsleeve, not a dirty hand.

After the small forward movement, I would then move to my left one sideways movement, and begin the search all over again. Geez, I thought: what happened to my hole location?

Suddenly the ground surface felt spongy. I slowly wiggled a finger into the ground and felt a hard surface a few inches below! I signaled to Mike that I had found a possible opening and would continue my search. I followed the edge of the hard surface that covered the entrance. It was something of a lid. I moved ever so slowly, so I wouldn't miss the feel of a trip-release wire or electrical contact. Checking the whole perimeter of the hard cover with my fingers, I slowly lifted one edge, but only high enough to slide one finger around the inner edge. I found no obstructions. I slid my flattened hand under the lid and searched its under surface areas. ...all clear. I lifted and removed the lid, revealing an opening barely visible by the moonlight. I continued feeling the inner surface of the opening, downward perhaps about a foot.

Suddenly my hand contacted a wire. My heart raced as any irregular movement of the wire could, in theory, kill Mike and me. One explosive experience, even through it was training, was enough. I gingerly followed the wire to a small wooden stake on the inside wall of the opening. I reached into my pocket and retrieved the plastic knife. I inserted the knife into the dirt and checked around the stake for possible buried explosives.

Nothing!

I slowly followed the wire back to the opposite end. My hand suddenly stopped as I felt a cold hard object. I had to concentrate to slow my breathing. The combination of fear, adrenalin, and anxiety all combined; had my hand a little shaky.

I palmed my hand around the object and recognized the feel of a hand grenade. I located the safety pin and got a tight grip on it. Holding the pin in place, I lifted the grenade and fully reinserted the safety pin, bending it over locking it in place. I called to Mike, showing him my prize. He smiled and gave me a thumbs up. I set the grenade aside and sat down for a break.

Mike motioned a mimed applause. Again, I continued my search of the hole and in a few minutes was totally inside the tunnel. I remember thinking: I've been in this hole a dozen times and never had a hard time breathing. Now I'm gasping for air. The ground even smells different. All I hear is my heart pounding like a diesel engine. I'm totally blind without any light.

I continue to ease myself forward, now laying on my stomach, concentrating—trying to feel anything, just anything. I estimated that I had gone nearly the length of the tunnel, and the end must surely be near. *Listen, did I hear something? Not really a noise, just a sense of something.* Just my heart again, I assumed.

No, I do hear something, but what? My heart is racing, my breathing deep and held back. I tried to listen, to hear anything.

There! I do hear something: very quiet, but rhythmic. Oh, damn. I hear someone breathing! What do I do now? Having no weapon I decided to go, "Bang, bang, you're dead!"

Suddenly and painfully, the tunnel was overwhelmed with light and I was temporarily blinded. Sergeant Miller exclaimed in a praising voice, "Great! Just great! I never knew you were there until you said bang. That was great!"

Getting accustomed to the light, Sarge, Mike and I patted each other's shoulders on a job well done. We had accomplished our mission. In the excitement, I exclaimed how I couldn't find the opening.

Sarge said, "That's because PFC Boykin and I moved the rock and made a new opening for this test. But you figured it out and did accomplish the mission. You survived, that's the whole lesson in this training."

I felt totally exhausted, but slept peacefully that night. That was an E-Ticket ride anywhere!

Mike Boykin, having completed explosive school, left for a tour of duty in Germany. I stayed for a three-day class on explosives and their use in underground demolition. Blowing dirt into the air was fun!

Sergeant Miler informed me that the base commander and Ordnance Control would like to visit our school for a demonstration. He said he had heard the budget was low and it looked like the school may be dissolved. He said I should arrange the camp so I could surprise the commander and his entourage by appearing from one of the holes as the enemy might do for a surprise attack.

He said," Why don't you check out some explosive and

set up the far bunker for an explosive demolition exhibition. You know how to do it, just set it up for a good show."

A good show? Well, I did "quarter-block" the bunker with T.N.T. The quarter block was enough to blow the bunker, but I wondered if it was enough to impress anyone. He did say "a good show" and I was determined to give them just that.

After an hour of continuous labor, I had the bunker set. I then linked the bunker to the long tunnel via D.E.T.-cord. This is an explosive cord, that will simultaneously explode a connected explosive. Next, I figured the grass hut would burn nicely so I connected it also.

The next morning at breakfast, Sarge asked how far I had gotten on the demonstration. I told him I had completed the preparations and he could expect an eye opening demonstration.

"Before the detonations, I'll wait for you to finish your speech on the tunnel rat program, jump from the camouflaged hole and show how the enemy uses it to conduct ambushes. We'll demonstrate its concealment by shooting at the audience with blank rounds."

Sarge said that should be a really big shock when I did that. I agreed it would be "a really, really, big shock".

XIV

A REALLY GOOD SHOW

I met Sarge at the training site. He asked, "Are the charges connected yet?"

I told him it was ready; I only needed to attach the arming device. I would have the detonating device ready for his use at the podium in front of the makeshift bleachers. I explained that while he gave a short tour of the training camp, I would hide myself in the hole in front of the bleachers with a cover on top of the hole.

We agreed that at the completion of his talk, "The History of Tunnel Rats and Tunnels," he would introduce me as the first trained tunnel rat. At that time, I would pop out from the hole pointing an AK-47 at the audience, hoping for such a shocked response that it would point out the necessity for keeping this school.

The invited guests began to arrive. There were a group of army reporters; some men from another training area, and some Special Forces officers interested in this line of training. The Post Commander, a one star general, and other officers arrived. Sarge very diplomatically welcomed them. After he conducted a short tour, all the guests took a seat in the portable bleachers and Sarge began his speech.

I had been in the hole for over fifteen minutes and was feeling a bit cramped. I hoped Sarge would talk faster, but it seemed that he acquired "talk-itis" and kept adding to his speech.
My legs were losing their feelings and it was hot and humid. Finally, Sarge ended his talk and introduced me.

"...and now, our first tunnel rat graduate of the U.S. Army

A Really Good Show

Tunnel Rat School, Private First-Class Steve Mendez."

I was ready, but my legs had cramped. I wiggled around to get feeling back into my legs. My muscles were tight and my circulation had been restricted. Sweat rolled down my face. Finally, I just threw up the camouflaged cover and popped out pointing the AK-47 at the audience. I fired several blank rounds into the air.

It was great! The Special Forces guy on the front seat fell backwards in shock. There were gasps of surprise and wide eyes. The audience then applauded and the General walked down and shook the Sarge's hand in congratulations. The General was still laughing as the Green Beret dusted himself off.

Sarge asked everyone to be seated for the demonstration of the destruction of an enemy bunker. He explained that even though we would locate and hopefully capture equipment or personnel, we would not leave the complexes usable to the enemy again. While the General offered words of praise and encouragement, I went to the bunker and began rolling out the electrical cord to attach to the plunger. The bunker and tunnel were about 300 feet from the bleachers. I handed the Sarge the plunger and said, "It's all ready."

Sarge, in a diplomatic jester, asked the General if he would honor this demonstration and first graduating class by pressing the plunger and destroying the enemy bunker. The General accepted and stepped to the podium. The General, taking the plunger in hand, turned to the audience and asked them to cover their ears: "Just for fun."

The General pressed the plunger.... The ground erupted with a loud crack, crash, and boom. The bunker, tunnel and hooch instantly disappeared in a cloud of dust and smoke. The General, a little stunned, turned with a smile on his face. He was a kid again, just having won a major battle. Victory! Most of the audience had almost fallen to the ground, not expecting such a large, loud explosion. The look on Sarge's face was worth a million bucks: surprise, shock and a look of total dismay. He turned to me with a look of, "what happened?"

The general said, "that was a—"

But before he could complete the sentence, the mass of dirt that had been blown upward into the sky, decided to begin falling. It fell all over the audience, and fell, and fell. While Sarge stood in shock, most of the crowd jumped from the bleachers and departed rather quickly, including the general and his staff.

A few of the Special Forces guys stayed to compliment us on the best show they've ever had seen. They especially liked our surprise enemy in the hole. The elder Special Forces sergeant said I was better than a real VC. He had been to Vietnam, so I took it as a high compliment.

Sarge looked at me and said, "I only told you to blow the bunker, not the whole damn state of Louisiana!"

Luckily for me, he began laughing and said for me to clean up the place and meet him back at the office. As I cleaned up the area, I felt a sense of real accomplishment. I reveled on the praise from the Special Forces guys. They really thought I was good ... and I felt good.

Later that day Sarge said he didn't think the school would be continued. He said that the general's office called and said the school is a needed training item and that he was very impressed by the demonstration. But, they said the funding wasn't included in the new training budget for Fort Polk. Sarge said my orders would be ready by the next day. I'd get my leave time and orders to a new unit. He said he would eventually be reassigned to another training area. I was saddened that the school would close. I liked Sarge and knew how he loved creating training challenges for young soldiers like me.

"I'm a soldier," he said when I mentioned how I felt. "I go where the army sends me."

We decided to have a dinner at the Enlisted Men's Club and celebrate the school's opening, graduation, and closing.

A Really Good Show

We had a good time discussing the school and his teachings. I did tell him I was concerned that my overzealous demonstration not only eliminated the school's bunkers and tunnels, but I may have influenced the general's decision by covering him with all that dirt.

Sarge said, "You know, I think that's the first time that general ever made a decision that fast. But the look on his and his staff's face with all that dirt on them was worth it all. I felt a little relief, knowing Sarge held no grudge against me. The next morning Sarge called me to this office.

"I have your orders," he said. "I really tried my best to get you a spot in a European unit, but it's just impossible. You're an infantryman. I wish you the best. Just remember: find those trip-wires before entering." Sarge then handed me a tiny package, wrapped as a present. He quickly interjected, "Don't think I expect anything; it's just something to remember me by; something you dropped back in school. Go ahead and open it."

I unwrapped the small present, stared at it, and turned it over in my hand. I told Sarge, "I guess this will really keep my mind on my purpose and job. Thanks." We shook hands. I turned and left the office walking back to my barracks. I lifted the present up to look at it again. It was the plastic knife I found and used in the night test. I didn't fully understand Sarge's deepest thoughts, but I knew that for me, they were good thoughts. He was a fine soldier, a credit to his profession.

As the plane hit some turbulence, I awakened and realized that I was still airborne. We would land very soon and hopefully feel like young men again. I looked around at my buddies. Some of them looked very solemn, others were looking out the plane's side windows. We were about to touch down on Vietnamese soil for the first time in more than thirty years. The plane landed on a patchwork of rough runway. It probably hadn't been resurfaced in many years. The flight attendant announced, "Welcome to Vietnam. We hope you have a pleasant and memorable visit."

The plane stopped and everyone stood up to leave. As the plane's door opened, letting in the bright sunshine, we were ushered down the aisle to the exit door. The first look out wasn't as moving a feeling as I expected. There were no Air Force planes, no masses of military soldiers. Times had certainly changed. Ton-Son Nhut, our major airport during the Vietnam War, was now just another crowded airport, carrying everyday civilians, businessmen, vacationers, and families meeting their relatives.

We walked down the stairway to the tarmac where a small entourage of Vietnamese diplomats greeted us. They informed us that General Toi had arranged for our transportation to Ho Chi Minh City's best hotel, "The Saigon Hilton." The ride through the city was interesting. Although there were more buildings, more bicycles, more motorcycles, more pedestrians, and more confusion; the city and the people seemed the same. They still wore the white and black silk pajamas. A straw conical hat adorned everyone's head. The young girls, with their long flowing black hair, were as beautiful as ever. The people smiled when they noticed our round eyes; some even waved. I smiled and waved back. Doc Barult, who had surprised us that he would come at all, said: "They still all look like VC to me. It's like we're in the back of a deuce-and-a-half riding through Tay Ninh again. I guess I should feel different now, but I can't."

Don Farmhouser clicked away with his camera. I'm sure he used a whole roll of film from the airport to the hotel. The hotel seemed as old as time itself. But it was clean and had window air conditioning. The rooms even had bottled water on the side table.

John Meddos spoke up saying, "I'm hungry!" It seemed that John was always hungry. But he was right, we all agreed. We needed something to eat. A Vietnamese diplomat informed us that a dinner was to be held in our honor that evening and a

A Really Good Show

tour guide was available downstairs for our needs. He would take us anywhere we wanted to go. We took a unanimous vote to just do our own guiding and look for a place to eat along the way. We walked the streets freely, experiencing no animosity from the people. We eventually stumbled upon a building that read, French-America Cuisine. "Let's try this place!" Gary exclaimed.

We entered to find a nice little restaurant with round tables and a well stocked bar. The menus were written in French. A man behind the bar spoke to us in French. Noticing our lack of understanding, he approached us and spoke a few German words. "Humm.... Nein," he said. Then he spoke some Russian words. When we failed to respond to that language, he raised his eyebrows, gesturing with his shoulders and his palms out.

Bob Tillis said, "We're Americans…"

"Well, why didn't you say so? Americans? G.I.s!" Were you here during the war?

"Yes" L.T. and others replied.

"Good" he said and smiled broadly. "Now I can raise my prices for the rich Americans." He laughed heartily and then announced: "The first drink is on me!" We had a good lunch and made small talk with the French owner. He was an interesting man with a shadowy past. He said he had lived in Vietnam all through the war. He seemed to have the highest regard for us and for all American G.I.s.

Sergeant Browning looked at his watch and said we should be leaving. We said our thanks and returned to the hotel. Inside the lobby, Larry Cunnings said, "I guess things really have changed. I'd like to visit the countryside, though. Maybe the good general could arrange a bus tour back to Tay Ninh City."

"Good general, my butt," Doc Barult scoffed.

XV

VIETNAM DINNER PARTY

*W*e spent an hour just remembering old times while preparing for our dinner date. Promptly at 6:00 p.m., an assistant to the general knocked on our door. He said that if we were all prepared to go, our rides were ready to take us to the general's home for the welcoming dinner. We all met in the hotel reception area.

Stuart Simmons joked about the last time he was in a Saigon hotel lobby: it was to hire a prostitute for the night. "Very expensive, but worth it," he said, and then laughed.

I told him I bet we could go to Tay Ninh and look up a girl we all knew as "Water Buffalo" if he wanted. We laughed again, confident in the peacefulness of our surroundings and certain of the hospitable intentions of our host.

We mounted a small shuttle bus, drove quickly to the city limits and down a one-lane road for another few miles. We were quiet, thinking about the past and enjoying the beautiful scenery. Roser broke the silence: "Hey look! Are those soldiers walking out there?"

We all moved to one side of the bus to take a look. Dave Whiteman said, "They sure are! And they still carry AK's. I wonder what's going on."

"Maybe they're on training maneuvers" Cunnings said.

Doc Barult asked the assistant riding with us, "Do you know what they're doing?"

"Yes," he replied eagerly. "They guard the area of the general's home. General Toi is a very important man. Please be ready… we are entering the general's property now."

Vietnam Dinner Party

The bus turned onto a stone covered driveway leading up to a large wooden home. In America, it might be considered a rustic family dwelling of average size. Here it was a mansion when compared to the homes we had seen. The house was painted in an oriental style, with many colors peculiar to the Vietnamese culture. The building was surely an old French structure, probably once belonging to a wealthy rubber plantation owner. We stopped at the entrance to the home. Large pillars stood beside the lavish entrance. Two very large teakwood doors were opened by a soldier to allow us to enter. He was obviously a sentry and he stood at attention as we passed.

When the doors were fully open, General Toi was standing inside the foyer in full dress military uniform. "Welcome Gentlemen, welcome," he said. "It is good to see you again. Please come in and have refreshments."

The home was elegantly decorated and furnished, adorned with the memorabilia of General Toi's family history and military mementos of every kind. He walked us through his home, obviously very proud of it. He entertained us with short stories about his family and his own military history. He told us of how sad it was that he had no relatives to follow his family military heritage.

John Meddos asked, "You don't have any family in Vietnam? None at all?"

"No," he replied. "My only nephew was killed during the war. I have no other relatives. But, let's not dwell on the past. Many dignitaries will arrive to meet you. This day will be a day of renewing our mutual histories."

Soon, several other well-dressed and distinguished persons arrived. A number of high ranking military personnel entered the house, also. Stuart Simmons remarked: "You would think he would have had plenty of news media people here to exploit a good humanitarian story."

"Maybe the general will have the newspaper and media

people in after the dinner," I suggested.

L.T. said he figured General Toi had to first arrange to secure our safety and the safety of his other guests. "That's probably just the way things are done here."

"The general must really be important with all this security around here," Sergeant Browning said. "I just went to the back side of the home ... checking things out. When I got to the back door, I could see soldiers in the back garden. I kept the door slightly open and looked around. I saw several military trucks and a couple of dozen soldiers. I guess they must be changing shifts or something."

"Dinner is served," a servant announced.

The General stood at the head of a long table in the large dining room; his dignitaries seated close to him. We were seated equally on each side of the table. General Toi was elaborately dressed, his uniform bedecked with dozens of medals and accoutrements. When we were seated, General Toi began:

"Gentlemen and fellow soldiers. Thank you for visiting our country. We have been divided too long. It's time we finally came together—no longer as soldiers at war—but to take hands in forgiveness. Only then can we and our ancestors rest comfortably. The future will show the finality of war on this visit. Bad memories and pain will finally come to rest!"

Bob Tillis said: "Whose memories is he talking about? I know my memories will always be there."

"Yeah!" Roser said. "And the finality of my war occurred when I went home in '70."

General Toi continued: "Let me welcome the secretary of security for this region." The security secretary reminded me of a character from a James Bond Movie. He appeared to be a devious oriental man, who might enjoy putting pins under your fingernails. He was short and very slim. His eyebrows had vanished long ago. He had thinly opened eyes—just slits—that made him appear very ominous, and, he was always shifting his stare from one of us to the other. I felt he would begin an interrogation at any moment.

"And this person," General Toi said, pointing to his left, "is my long time friend. He served as a troop commander under me during the war. The closest person to family I have. Now let me welcome to our country the brave and gallant soldiers from America. Men, who like myself, fought in the name of freedom. They are here as our honored guests. Welcome, Gentlemen!" The Vietnamese guests and our guys applauded to each other in mutual recognition.

The dinner was great. The wine flowed freely and small talk between guests improved and continued unabated. Everyone was courteous to one another. Near the completion of the main course, the general stood up. "Gentlemen and fellow soldiers, Let me propose a toast. To all who have fought and died in the past, we hope this reunion will rest the souls of their ancestors."

We raised a glass and drank to his toast. We then went to another meeting room, somewhat like a library. This room was decorated only in military memorabilia. The general, seeing most of us studying the pictures of soldiers during the Vietnam War, asked if we had such items in our homes.

I replied, "Yes, I was proud to be a soldier and I have a few items and pictures I reminisce with. We have reunions and use pictures to remind our failing memories of the hardships, but also the friendship we had for each other. The soldiers we served with become a lifelong memory; the same as the hardship of losing some of those friends."

"Yes, Yes!" General Toi exploded. "I have those same memories ... the glory of battle and the terrible loss of a friend or relative."

"Hey guys," Dave Whiteman said. "Look at this picture. This base camp photo with the mountain in back! Don't you think it looks like Nui Ba Den mountain?"

We all gathered around the photo, each giving our opinion. John Meddos said, "Well, if that's Nui Ba Den, is that base camp Fire Support Base Washington?"

Now we all really began studying the photo. The mountain seemed right. The base camp looked familiar, but the photo was taken from an angle we hadn't seen before. Dave Whiteman said, "Hey Sarge, you were there the longest, can you tell?"

"It looks like Washington," Sarge said. "But it's been a long time.... Why don't you ask the general?"

General Toi and L.T. had been in a discussion about leadership in our different Armies. L.T. noticed our group looking his way and gave us a questioning look. Whiteman beckoned him to bring the general to our area. L.T. asked General Toi to come and see what interested the other men so much. They walked over to us. "Gentlemen, does this collection of photos interest you?" General Toi asked.

"Well, yes," Dave Whiteman said. "This picture here has us guessing if we recognize the mountain and camp. Could this be "Nui Ba Den, the Black Virgin Mountain? And perhaps the base camp in the foreground is "Fire Support Base Washington," in Tay Ninh Province?"

"Yes ... indeed that is Nui Ba Den. The base camp is the one you called Washington. But we called it "number ten" because of the fierce fighting American solders who were there. I did admire those soldiers. They always fought hard and brave. I made extra effort to avoid contact with them. Maybe someday they too, would like to also visit our country again."

We just couldn't believe the coincidence of us seeing our own base camp from a photo taken by the enemy. Now the onetime enemy was our host and had "our" memory hanging on his wall. We stood in front of the picture, pointing to a bunker and recognizing it as one we had slept in ... lived in.

Lieutenant Schmitter and Sarge were surprised at his collection of photos. They too realized that the photos were of places where we had patrolled and fought several battles.
We all wanted to ask the general more direct questions, but L.T. said we should be prudent and wait for another time.

John Meddos said, "Well, let's ask if we could arrange a ride to Tay Ninh and revisit the area. What do you guys think?" Discussing the idea very briefly, we decided to approach the general.

General Toi found the proposal more than acceptable. "Wonderful," he said "It would be a pleasure to reunite you with a familiar area of our country. Yes, Tay Ninh. I myself am familiar with this area. I have a good friend still serving that area. I'll contact him and make arrangements immediately."

We were all lost in small talk of possibly revisiting a battle zone. We had lost some good friends in that area and it held so many memories. "Hey Meddos," Doc Barult said. "Isn't that the area where Gary Standish got a leg wound when he was in a tunnel with Shortround?"

John replied: "Yup, I'm sure it is. It would have been me with Shorty if I hadn't been trying to take ammo to Whiteman for his M-60."

We finished our drinks and felt it time to head back to the hotel. The General, always the perfect host, was at the door shaking each man's hand and thanking them for honoring his home with their presence. As we took our seats on the bus, General Toi entered. He stood at the front next to the driver. "Wonderful news," he said. "I just received a phone call back from my friend in Tay Ninh. He can make the visiting arrangements and I can provide transportation. I'm embarrassed to ask you this, but my resources allow me no other choice. If we make this visit to Tay Ninh, I can only provide the use of a deuce-and-a-half truck. This would be an uncomfortable trip, but possible. I will let you discuss this among yourselves."

"I think I can speak for the guys," L.T. said. "We would all like to go, even if we had to walk. We would appreciate any arrangements you can provide."

We all indicated our approval with loud and excited cheers.

"Then until tomorrow, I say good night," General Toi said and bowed. "I'll assume you will all make the trip tomorrow?

I'll meet with you gentlemen in the morning with more information." As the general exited the bus, two armed soldiers entered and seated themselves in the front.

"I guess they still have that curfew and we'll need the guards for safe passage back to the hotel," Sarge said.

"I just don't like all these soldiers around," Doc Barult commented. "It makes me feel like a mouse in a cage... trapped."

"Aw, come on Doc, just loosen up and try and enjoy yourself," Bob Tillis said as he slapped Doc on the back.

"Yeah, I guess I should," Doc agreed. "Do you really think they still have the curfew where everyone had to be off all streets by 10:00 p.m. or be considered an enemy?"

"It's possible," L.T. answered. "This government is still a communist style regime. Curfews would be the norm."

On the trip back to the hotel, we quizzed each other on our memories of the Tay Ninh area. We talked about the many combat situations we had encountered and we laughed at the dumb things we had done. We all were anxious to see how the area might have changed. We contemplated the thought of climbing Nui Ba Den, but looking at the size of some of my friend's belt lines, we dismissed the thought of a 3,000-foot rocky climb, even by stairs.

We reminisced about the two missions we did have on Nui Ba Den. They were hard days of rock to rock jumping—never an easy trail—just a giant pile of granite stone boulders. The mountain sloped to a saddle, and rose again to a smaller mountain called Nui Cai. We sure found plenty of enemy while on a mission there.

***W*e had spent four days trying to locate the enemy and** his hiding place. The mission began at the top. An American radio command center was located there. The enemy wanted it out, so they constantly harassed the radio station, trying to convince the army to remove it, but it stayed.

Vietnam Dinner Party

Those four days of jumping from boulder to boulder was hard on the knees. Making it even harder and more dangerous was the weight of our backpacks. We had three days of food, water, ammunition and other items crammed into the pack. It wasn't unusual for a backpack to weigh over a hundred pounds. I do remember times when the weight actually exceeded my physical abilities. I was lucky enough to have such great men with me who would walk over to my pack and without question, remove a claymore mine, or pull out a few boxes of C-rations and add them to their own weight. Their thoughtfulness was humbling. They were my friends ... my family. I always think of them and how thankful I was for them. I could laugh at my own shortcomings. Ha! It seems Gary Standish always carried extra weight for me. What a great friend he was to me.

The fourth day was supposed to end this mission. As we worked our way down the edge of the saddle, we came under heavy enemy fire. A few anxious moments passed as we arranged our company into a protective position. We returned small arms fire for most of the day. Our food and water supply was almost depleted, and the heat of the glaring sun forced us to seek shade.

Our captain had arranged for a badly needed helicopter resupply of food, ammunition, and water. We had wounded men that needed evacuation and hospital attention. In short, this was a lousy day.

The helicopter arrived and began to push supplies out of its side door. The supplies crashed down on the rocks below, some falling between the boulders, unable to be retrieved. Then, "WHAM," an RPG rocket hit the tail of the helicopter. It spun in a circle. The exceptionally skilled pilot gained what little control he had of it and flew it like a crooked snake, headed towards the mountain's bottom. A trail of white smoke followed him down.

We all watched, holding our collective breaths. We knew those guys. The chopper landed hard in the green brush down at the mountain bottom. Gratefully, we could see the men exit the aircraft safely. A few minutes later the bird exploded and burned to a pile of molten metal.

We scurried over and between the rocks to retrieve as much of the re-supply as possible. The food and water was sparingly distributed. Some men bartered for a can of fruit for its liquid contents. We were nearly dehydrated from lack of water and lying in the heat all day. The tense situation wore on us, draining our energy. Everyone constantly shifted around during the day to find shade wherever he could. As night slowly ascended, the temperatures fell. It felt nice at first, but we forgot about being high on the mountain. The temperature got to about 60 degrees. That's freezing when you're not prepared and in the open air.

The heat during the day caused us to huddle close to the boulders for shade. Now at night, those same boulders radiated the warmth they had absorbed from the day's heat and they kept us a little warmer. As we watched for any movement on the mountain, we noticed glowing embers among the distant boulders. As the minutes passed, we could tell the glow of a certain ember would slowly change its location. The word was passed to stay alert as information of the glowing embers circulated among the other soldiers.

The night was cold and long. Luckily, the enemy must have taken shelter from the cold night air as we had. The embers slowly faded until we saw no more. Standish, Sarge, and I were keeping watch by a large boulder as daybreak arrived. The sun's rays felt good, removing some of the night's chill. The word was passed that our artillery support was moving up to the base of the mountain and later we might have an air strike.

As we prepared for the impending attack, I told Sarge, "I'm going to crawl down that space next to the large boulder to make sure no one can surprise us by climbing up from it."

Sarge said, "Ok, but let the others know about it."

I passed the word that I was preparing to go down under

the rocks. John Meddos asked, "Shortround, do you need any help?"

"Sure," I said. "Wait here and if I need anything I'll call back to you, okay?"

"Great, just call," John said. He was always a helping hand to me and he helped make my job much easier.

The space between the boulders was cool and damp, quite unlike a dirt tunnel. The boulders were tightly spaced, only allowing me to slide down between them with hardly an inch of space to spare. I passed from one boulder to the next one and was able to stand erect. But it was also dark with not much light filtering down. I continued sideways for a while, and then I went deeper. I continued on, trying to hear any evidence of the enemy.

I wanted to get as close as possible to them. Maybe I could get a good location on them and their size. I couldn't chance a fight; I only had my .45-caliber pistol with me and no extra ammunition. My watch showed its glowing dots and I determined that I had been down about one hour. I could feel the coolness and I was thirsty. I allowed myself a rest before heading any farther. I lay back on a flat, angled boulder with my left hand against the last rock I'd climbed down. Holding on to the rock helped me to maintain my direction.

I thought it very unusual that I could smell smoke. The smell became a little thicker and I thought I heard pebbles fall. My heart almost stopped as I noticed a slight red glow ahead of me. I sat up to see that it was increasing in size. I sat motionless and stared intently. The glow became a flicker of sparks. Someone was blowing on a burning ember at the end of a stick. When the ember glowed bright red, the person moved around the boulder in front of me and disappeared. Then another glowing stick appeared. I knew immediately the enemy was searching the same as I was.

I slowly and gently pulled myself back up the boulder and then up the next boulder. After each climb, I stopped. I listened intently for any sound of being followed or the smell of smoke from their glowing sticks. When I was absolutely sure it was safe, I continued up and over another rough boulder.

At each large stone, I climbed more urgently to reach the top and with each boulder, I gained an increasing degree of sunlight. As I cleared the last boulder, I could see John Meddos peering down with squinted eyes, hoping it was me making the noise. When he recognized me, he quickly reached down a hand to help me up and out. "Thanks," I said. "Hand me a canteen."

John frantically questioned me. "Wud ya see, Wud ya see." I held my hand for him to stop asking questions while I satisfied my thirst.

"I saw enough," I gasped. "Tell Sarge to come over." John motioned, waving Sarge over to our rock.

"Where have you been, to China?" Sarge asked. He chuckled lightly. He new I was good at my job—maybe a little crazy—but dependable.

"I went deep and pretty far ahead," I said "They're out there. They even passed within a few feet from me. They're using coal, burning at the end of sticks, as light to get through the rock openings down there. They were doing that last night. I think they're looking to get closer to us so we need extra sentries watching for movement."

Sarge went to each of his lookout positions and explained what I had seen. Hopefully, the enemy hadn't found a place to sneak through the rocks. The morning remained quiet until a few guys tried climbing to a higher boulder for a better position. Crack! Crack! Crack! The sound of several AK-47s sent us all behind my rock for protection.

No one was hurt. The tension mounted as the commanding officer passed the word by radio that artillery support was incoming. A few seconds passed. Then we could hear the rushing, high-pitched sound of the incoming artillery rounds. KA-WOHMP! They pounded the boulders heavily. We saw a group of four 155-MM howitzers mounted on track carriers at the mountain's base firing upwards. We could see the puff of smoke exhale from the barrel's ends as they fired. The rounds would explode seconds later, only a hundred yards away. Shards of stone would rain down like hail after each explosion. They pounded the enemy for several minutes.

The barrage lifted and all was deadly quiet. We meekly peeked over the protective boulders to see the damage or to locate any enemy kills. We could see the haze hanging over the boulders and smell the smoke. We thought maybe we'd defeated them or they hid themselves away, not wanting any more from the artillery.

Suddenly, the crack, crack, crack of the AK-47s began again, spraying bullets everywhere. Most of the rounds ricocheted off the rocks. The enemy had a secure place for protection and they weren't leaving any time soon. The artillery had hardly damaged their hiding places and they knew they had the advantage. For several more hours we exchanged pop shots at each other, not knowing if either side was causing injury or was gaining any advantage.

In mid-afternoon an air strike flew over, dropping 500-pound bombs. It was awesome seeing Phantom jets fly in towards the mountain face—seeming to come straight at us. At the very last moment they would pull up and bank off to one side or the other. Their bombs struck the mountain side exploding like a horrible thunder. I wondered how the enemy could survive such firepower. The explosions even caused us to vibrate on top of the boulders. It was so intense; it hurt our bodies with the concussions.

Finally, we were given orders to pack up and head downhill during the next bombing attack. We were all thrilled to pull off the mountain; we really needed the rest. My thoughts drifted back to the present as a pothole jarred the bus. We were headed back to Nui Ba Den, the site of my idle dreaming.

The trip thus far was enjoyable and the rest of the guys

began to loosen up a little. Doc was a lot more at ease and even said the general wasn't what he expected. Maybe this reunion would help mend bad memories, some of them to take home and pass on to our other veteran friends.

The bus was only a few miles from town when Larry Cunnings asked the driver if we could make a pit stop. The two soldiers at the front rejected Larry's request. We spoke up and motioned that others of us would also like to stop. Finally, the soldiers told the driver to stop. We exited the bus and walked to the edge of the dirt road. I looked up to see a sky full of brightly lit stars. I thought how I hadn't remembered really seeing them during the many, many nights I spent sleeping in the boonies. I could remember how the ground smelled. I could even remember that Ben Soi smelled different than other areas. One place would smell like black dirt from back home in Wisconsin, while other areas smelled of rotted, moldy swamp.

I can say that there was no water that ever tasted as good as the water back home. We usually put purification tablets in the stagnant water of Vietnam, making it taste bad. We knew any water taken from rivers or ponds would make us ill. There were times we did drink water so badly discolored we couldn't really tell it was water; especially water taken from a bomb crater. Remembering was our whole connection to this trip. We all had differing degrees of recollection and a lot of bad memories, but we found ways to turn each bad situation into a funny story.

We usually asked each other or a certain buddy—about a particular firefight or a rest and relaxation stand-down, beginning the question with: "Do you remember…?" And the memories continued.

It was very reassuring to talk to your old friends as they could reaffirm your memory. After so many years, I sometimes wondered if I was really remembering the moments of my tour accurately. The photos we cherished and held so dear also help our memories, especially as the passing years changed our appearance. We had gone from virile and fit young men to overweight and balding fathers or grandfathers. Time is always cruel, isn't it?

One of the guards began speaking loudly at the back of the bus. We all walked around to the rear and were surprised to see a small boy holding a rope connected to a large water buffalo. It seemed the guard was angry because the young boy asked for water to drink. The guard was ordering the boy to take his buffalo and leave.

When the guard pointed his rifle at the boy's pet, Sarge stepped up between the guard and boy, holding up his hands and motioning to the guard to calm down. He handed the boy a bottle of water we had brought along. The boy smiled and said words in Vietnamese that didn't need any translation.

The guard was really angry and ordered us back onto the bus. I guess Sarge must have a little politician in him because as he entered the bus he gave the guard a few bills of money. The guard didn't respond until Sarge reached out a hand to shake. The guards spoke a few words, then smiled and sat down. The drive back to the hotel was casual with plenty of chitchat.

As I lay in the hotel bed trying to sleep, my mind constantly flipped through the pages of my combat tour. Tomorrow's trip to Tay Ninh would be the excursion I had imagined many times before. Would my feelings of difficult, hot days—humping endless miles—the sweat always soaking my body, come back to me? I remembered days so hot and humid as to dehydrate a soldier long before the sun reached the middle of the sky. I remembered my nerves on edge constantly, and ending the long days only to have to go out at night and set up platoon ambushes. At night you laid on the ground to sleep, but only until someone shook you awake, handing you a borrowed watch and saying: "Hey man, it's your turn for watch."

Your body and your mind both ached—you struggled through sleep-dried eyes to try peering into the darkness of dense jungle. You could see nothing. You remember how hard it was to recognize any shapes, but your mind did a still photo of patterns to your front and sides. Every few minutes you stared to see if that still photo had added or deleted any objects, suggesting something or someone had entered or left the photo implant. You constantly looked at the glowing dots of the watch, hoping the hands had moved closer to your end of guard duty.

Somehow, time goes in slow motion when you are on watch. The clock is the only thing that creeps forward in time. All the while, those relentless mosquitoes buzzed around your poncho-liner covered head. Sometimes the buzzing was so tormenting that you wanted to just jump up and scream. But survival was our most important concern. You just sat motionless, hoping you didn't see or hear anything. You learned how quiet, quiet can be. Finally, the glowing dots of the watch showed an end to your guard time. You crawled over the dirt and brush to locate your buddy laying just a few feet away. You shake him awake with the usual greeting: "Hey man, it's your turn for watch!"

You leave him, believing that he'll stay awake and protect you while you doze. You crawl back to your dirt bed and with no hesitation fall asleep. You trust him.

My eyes opened wide, and being unsure of my surroundings, I jerked myself to an upright sitting position. My anxiety quickly eases as I realize that I'm sitting on a bed in the hotel room. I notice my body is covered in sweat from my dreams.

I joined the rest of our group at breakfast. We were all anxious to hear from the general as to what type of tour we could expect and how long it would last. He arrived with several other men just as we were finishing our meal. We invited them to join us for coffee. General Toi sat at the front end of the table and gained our attention.

General Toi began: "Today gentlemen, we will begin our

adventure by revisiting an area you are so familiar with. I hope it provides you with great memories. We have arranged for the trucks to take you there. You will be met by my friend in Tay Ninh. He has made accommodations for you there to refresh yourselves before a tour of the city and the War Museum. Then after a restful night's sleep, I will join you for a special tour, which I have arranged personally. I'm sure you will be overwhelmed with feelings of comradeship and honor. Enjoy yourselves today. Tomorrow we will see past history revisited!" The general excused himself with what he called "military obligations."

Bob Tillis said, "War Museum? I bet everything in it will be American made." His comment brought a chuckle from the rest of us.

"Okay guys," L.T. interrupted. "I'm sure it'll really be interesting. Now, most of you guys will get to see the other end of what was firing back at you. I'd like to get a close look at one of those RPG launchers. We sure know the receiving end of that gun!"

Larry Cunnings said, "L.T.'s right. I bet we'll really see some neat stuff there."

"Sounds good to me," Stuart Simmons said. "Does anyone have any idea what his personal tour is about?"

"Yeah," Doc said. He also said things like comradeship and honor. I bet he plans on having news people there. Maybe he's arranging things at the war museum we're visiting."

"A truck is pulling up out in front," I said. "I hope it doesn't get too hot on the way." We all boarded the truck, just as we did back in basic training. The same two guards accompanied us to Tay Ninh. The ride was bumpy, but the roads were better than thirty years before. They were mostly blacktop roads through the cities, turning to dirt as we entered the countryside. The engineer crews we had in Vietnam during the war were always busy sweeping the roads for mines and keeping them open for supplies and troop movement. They saved plenty of lives doing that dangerous job.

The countryside hadn't changed much. We saw endless acreage of rice paddies. Farmers and families were knee deep in mucky, muddy water, tending to their rice crops. Some were bent over planting and weeding, while others followed their indigenous tractor; the "Water Buffalo."

Gary said, "Hey guys, that water buffalo reminds me of the night we were on ambush north of Fire Base Washington. Remember? We thought a whole battalion was coming our way."

Dave Whiteman chimed in: "When we thought they were close enough, we opened up with everything we had. The firebase even provided 105s for support. When the fighting ended and the sun came up, we did an area search for body count. To our surprise, the only casualties we found were a small herd of water buffalo!"

We all laughed, remembering the incident. We realized that weird, comical things did happen on our missions at times. We had many "remember this and remember that" along with exaggerated stories until we got within sight of Tay Ninh City.

"Okay guys," Sarge said. "Keep your eyes open for that Shell gas station." The Shell gas station was a tiny, one pump station on the dirt main street when we were there. The main road from Tay Ninh base came through a very small village en route to other field bases.

Whenever we were trucked through the city northward, we would see this icon of "home"—a connection to family and friends back in the "world." I believe every guy who ever passed through Tay Ninh has a photo of it: A Shell gas station with only one pump and a brightly painted "Shell" sign.

In a matter of minutes we had driven from one side of the town, exiting the other side. We knew it was just a short distance to the Tay Ninh base camp entrance. As we drove down the road, the villagers gawked at us as we passed with the same familiar bland stare we saw years before. A few of the younger ones would wave at us and yell in Vietnamese. We waved back.

Vietnam Dinner Party

We turned off the main road and were pleasingly surprised to see a stately mansion. The truck lurched to a stop in front of a fountain. We all jumped down and walked towards the building. This ornate manor, with its manicured grounds, was really out of place as compared to the surrounding area. The big doors opened and a man came out wearing a wide smile.

Mr. Van, our guide, said, "Welcome, welcome. I hope your trip was pleasant. Come in and enjoy a cool drink. My friend, General Toi has told me interesting things about our American guests." He shook each of our hands as we entered his home.

"I have arranged a pleasant visit in the city for you. I'm sure many things have changed from your last visit. You will find the new museum quite rewarding. It has much information and history. Then we will return for a great feast in honor of your visit here."

As he finished his prepared greeting, a small bus pulled up in place of the truck. Gary said, "I sure hope the bus has more suspension than the truck."

We arrived at the museum to find that it had been a building used in our old base camp for a chapel. The outside entrance displayed several pieces of weaponry used during the war. Again, we looked down the barrel of a .51-caliber machine gun. They were a very destructive weapon as our experiences had proven.

The museum was not unlike other military museums. Displays of uniforms, weapons, and battle scene photos—taken through the camera's eye from our enemy's perspective—were hung everywhere. The photos were quite unusual to see. The soldiers were in all types of dress: some in NVA uniforms—others dressed in a mixture of uniform parts and farmer-style black pajamas. They wore the standard conical straw hat—not unlike the common local rice farmer—except most of them held AK-47 rifles instead of a hoe.

Sarge and L.T. were discussing a diagram map of an infiltration route used by the NVA to enter South Vietnam.

The rest of us found numerous photos of the vast tunnel complexes the NVA and VC had built during both the French and American occupations.

"Look at this!" Bob Tillis exclaimed. "That photo looks like Shorty! I could swear there's a picture of you over here." Everyone gathered around a series of photos and articles written in Vietnamese. As I looked over the photos, a cold chill ran down my back.

Gary insisted: "That sure is you, Shorty. I don't recall the area but that's surely you coming out of that tunnel." We studied the photos again and were able to recognize several other guys in photos of recovered arms and ammunitions. We called to our museum guide and asked if he would interpret the articles for us.

The guide complied saying in a heavy Vietnamese accent, "The article describes how American soldiers, upon discovering a tunnel or bunker, would send inside a selected soldier who was trained in killing soldiers hiding in tunnels or caves ... before having a chance to surrender peacefully."

I grunted sarcastically, hearing him read, "surrender peacefully."

The guide continued describing how the American "murderers" would call the revolutionary patriot to expose himself, and then merciless execute the surrendering patriot. We all let out an exclamation of resentment at those words.

Of course, we all knew by personal experience the truth about our actions. We had asked for this interpretation, and we were now a captive audience. We had to stand there and listen to our guide describe how terrible we were in their eyes and how well they could make an incident of war into personal executions; making us murderers in the "people's" minds.

I now recognized fully how propaganda could be used as a powerful tool against unknowing people. "The communists used these half-truths very well," I said. "The people had only propaganda as their news source."

Vietnam Dinner Party

My friends nodded in agreement, but the guide—who surely understood—simply grinned a plastic smile.

We left Vietnam after our tours were over, not being able to speak in our own defense or give our own thoughts—either as a soldier or civilian. Would the Vietnamese people ever understand that just as their very own soldiers were only schoolboys, they were very much like us? We had only known school, then war. The young men in these museum photos were not unlike us. They either didn't have a choice about the war, or they volunteered because they thought it was a just cause.

Yes, I volunteered for the service. I even became a tunnel rat by choice. It was a job I fit right in to. I was easy to convince that I was special: someone to be selected ahead of others and specially trained. I felt that I *was* special. I couldn't see my larger buddies fitting into those tight tunnels.

The photos did suggest a time when our group had discovered a tunnel complex near the Bo Loi woods area. We had encountered small groups of VC throughout a week of patrols. They would make contact with us, but break and run once our firepower descended upon them. We knew that we must be close to an enemy encampment or supply area to encounter them time after time.

On the fifth day out, we found a small enemy base camp. The camp was vacant but showed signs of recent use. We realized that they must have left quickly, as we found small amounts of rice in several bunkers and some recently cooked food. L.T. had us set up a quick perimeter and we began a thorough search of the area. We split up into small search groups to check the many bunkers. Any one of them might contain an enemy soldier or it could be booby-trapped. Each group searched thoroughly, and luckily, nothing harmful was found. With the camp secured, we sat down to rest before moving on.

Journey Into Darkness

The point squad radioed to L.T. that they found a possible tunnel. L.T. called for me to come ahead and evaluate the hole. I arrived at the hole to see the point squad guys standing a few feet away from an uncovered hole in the ground. "Guess what we found for you?" Tillis said.

Larry Cunnings said, "Hey Rat-Man, the hole looks well used. I get first dibs on a Chicom pistol." (A Chinese made automatic firearm, a rare and highly prized souvenir).

"You'll be lucky if I find some chopsticks," I replied with a light laugh. I began my job of searching the opening for any warning of booby traps. I found none. "Okay guys, I'm going in," I said.

I pulled off all unnecessary field gear. I carried only my .22-caliber Ruger pistol with shaved-head bullets, a flashlight my mom had sent me (a K-Mart chrome special), and my plastic knife. I laid aside my very powerful .45-caliber pistol to avoid the concussion headaches it caused; the .22-caliber was just as deadly.

Standish held on to my ankles as I went in headfirst. The tunnel went straight down approximately three feet and then angled away. When my head cleared the bottom, I signaled Gary to release his hold. I slid the final foot down, and pulled and crawled a few feet into the level portion of the tunnel.

The tunnel was well dug. It measured about three feet high and two feet wide. I lay there gathering my thoughts, trying to listen into the darkness. Not sure of the tunnel's purpose or if it might be occupied, I kept my flash light off. If I turned on the light before making an evaluation of my next moves, I would instantly show myself and alert anyone inside I was coming. They would know soon enough, anyway.

I sat up in a duck walk position and slowly moved forward in the dark. Every sense I had was measuring the tunnel's smell, temperature and texture. It was black as coal inside ... not even a sliver of light filtered from the opening. I had gone maybe only fifteen feet when a muffled "thud" vibrated the walls of the tunnel. It was like sitting inside a vacuum cleaner bag and having someone knock all the dirt and dust loose. I fell onto my belly when a heavier "thud" shook the tunnel like an earthquake. I began to choke and cough from the heavy dust in the confined space.

I figured that if anyone were inside with me, they would have done something after that shakeup. I turned on the flashlight only to see a gray haze. The light didn't help in the heavy dust. My eyes blinked rapidly to wash out the dirt that was grinding in my eyes. My lungs tightened from the thick dust I breathed. I turned around using the walls to touch for direction, and then half crawled and duck-walked my way back to the opening. My knees touched loose ground as my hands felt a pile of dirt ahead of me. I tried my flashlight again, but still, the dust prevented it from having any effect.

I kept reaching forward and to the sides, but only felt loose dirt. I soon realized the tunnel opening had collapsed. I was bewildered for a moment. Then the reality hit home. The guys above were in contact and the shakes I felt were incoming artillery. The explosions caused the tunnel entrance to collapse, trapping me inside!

I dug forward for a minute, and then stopped. I realized that my frantic digging would only cause me to use up my air supply. I lay down and tried to slow my breathing. I felt several more vibrations but they seemed weaker or more distant. I knew I could rely on my buddies above to dig me free when they had the chance.

I hadn't realized until I wiped my face with my shirtsleeve that I was drenched in sweat. The stale, dusty air, combined with a little fear, caused me to just pour sweat. *I sure could use some water.*

I had to think—think about keeping calm—think how lucky I was to be safe inside the tunnel away from the artillery, or, my weird version of thinking I was safe. I began to worry more as seconds became like hours. I hadn't heard or felt anything for a long time. *When will I hear them digging out the opening?*

A certain fear set in, thinking I might be forgotten in the heat of the battle above. Were my buddies safe? Were they still alive? Panic overcame me for a few moments. I turned on the flashlight and began digging. After several minutes of clawing, I became physically exhausted. I collapsed onto my back and struggled to breathe. *What should I do?* Then I thought to myself: *You dummy ... try going deeper inside and look for something to dig with.*

I crawled on my hands and knees, not fearing anymore for my safety. I reached an area that turned to my left, only to crawl a few more feet to a dead end. Not even a stick to help dig with! I lay there exhausted and smelling my own sweat, cursing my bad luck.

I pulled myself along back towards the opening. Somewhere during my crawl, I must have stopped to rest, only to succumb to exhaustion and thirst. I fell asleep. I didn't know how long I slept, but I'm sure it was for only a few minutes. My eyes tried to open, but resisted because of the irritation of dust and dirt in them. I felt a coolness rush onto my face, bringing me alert. I reached for my pistol. It was missing! Damn, I thought in a panic. I must have dropped it when I fell asleep. I frantically moved my hands around the dirt and located it. I held it, ready to use it if necessary. Something was happening that I could only sense—not see or hear—signaling me to a clear danger. I couldn't recognize it in my tired, scared state of mind. Then suddenly a blinding light filtered through the dust. I realized someone was digging into the tunnel!

Panic gripped me to the core. I became lost in my mind. I had nowhere to go. I surely couldn't hide. All I could do was watch as the opening was slowly cleared away and the digging instrument hit into the dirt, widening the hole.

At the very moment when I felt surely a Chicom grenade would come rolling in, I heard someone shout, "Hey Shortshit, you still in there or what?"

Vietnam Dinner Party

I fell squarely back onto my butt. I began to laugh amid the tears. There was John Meddos' goofy mustached smile, lit up by my flashlight. I reached out my hand and he grasped it. He pulled me through the loose dirt and out to the opening they had dug. All I could manage was a weak smile and held up my fingers in the "V" sign for victory.

The guys came over and patted my shoulder, and then handed me a canteen of water. Larry Cunnings came over and sat beside me. "Well!" he said. "Where's my souvenir?"

All I could reply with was a smile and, "Maybe next time." He rubbed my dirty head and said we were to be picked up at a nearby landing zone and head back to base camp. He said they were going to level the area with artillery after we left. I was ready to go.

Bob Tillis slapped me on my shoulder, bringing me back to reality and to the photos in the Tay Ninh museum. "Damn, Shorty," he said. "Someone must have snapped your picture for the VC. You're lucky they didn't have a bounty on your ass back then."

The guide said, "This article does state that many soldiers feared the 'Men of The Tunnels' ... the ones you call 'Tunnel Rats.' It states that many did have bounties, but none had been caught. To this very day, these men are respected and cursed. Our great hero, General Toi, had his only nephew killed when he was left to guard such a tunnel complex during the war."

"We lost a lot of men ourselves at some of these complexes," L.T. said. I guess we all have sad loses from the war."

We enjoyed the tour and thanked the guide for his help in translating. We were all hungry and ready for some food and a few beers. Our host greeted us as before, saying we should refresh ourselves and rest briefly before dinner. He said General Toi would join us and would have entertainment during the meal.

The early evening began to cool down as we all assembled in the library of the home for pre-dinner drinks. General Toi arrived and joined us. "Ah! Here we are all together again. I hope your day was pleasurable? Let's all enjoy ourselves with a drink." We hoisted a drink for all those who were in the war, both sides.

The dinner was the usual meat and potatoes, with plenty of vegetables. Mostly we just hoped that the meat was beef. It didn't look like anything I had seen before, but we all seemed to enjoy it. Larry Cunnings insisted the steaks were "water buffalo." The General said, "I have contacted a local musical group to play for your entertainment. Shall we go out to the gardens for more drinks and music?"

We were surprised. The musical group was a Vietnamese band providing a good imitation of an American rock band of the sixties. We all talked about our mutual interests and enjoyed our drinks. Eventually the band ended their playing and departed.

General Toi commented: "Gentlemen, you will reside here tonight. Tomorrow I have arranged a tour of our beautiful countryside. It will surely jolt your memories. This comes as a surprise, I'm sure. Therefore, I have taken the liberty of providing your rooms, each with a set of American fatigue uniforms. You will not have to worry about damaging them as they were left behind many years ago.

We all laughed knowing we'd probably finally find the fatigues our supply sergeant lost when he sent out our laundry to be washed, thirty years before.

XVI

PAYBACK

The next morning we were amused when we met for breakfast dressed in old army fatigues, but wearing tennis shoes and baseball caps. Larry Cunnings sure didn't look like he did thirty years before; nor did any of us. I wondered if Larry was able to button the waistband on his pants. All we could do was point and laugh at ourselves. The truck met us at the entrance of the mansion.

"I sure hope this field tour isn't far away," John Meddos said. "My butt is still sore from the last ride."

The truck had driven barely a half hour when it pulled off the road and into a field. We exited the truck and were surprised to hear a helicopter approaching. The chopper landed at the edge of the field as the truck driver motioned us out to the idling aircraft. Sarge yelled, "Come on guys ... just like the old days, remember?"

Yes, we all remembered, and like a bunch of high school boys, we all climbed aboard. I could see Doc was a little nervous, but most of us had smiles on our faces. "Let's take plenty of pictures for the next reunion, they'll never believe this one," Don Farmhouser shouted over the sounds of the whirling blades.

The helicopter, an American made Huey, lifted off, leaving me with a queasy feeling that I had long forgotten. It vanished quickly as I had always enjoyed an airlift. The chopper flew north for about twenty-five minutes and we enjoyed viewing the countryside from above. Even after all these years, we could still see evidence of bomb craters. The landscape was an emerald green of tropical lushness, unlike the stark gray nakedness caused by the "Agent Orange" chemical sprayed on miles of foliage.

We flew over the landscape, seeing the rice paddies and the sun reflecting off the water in the rice fields. It made a very nice picture. We flew past Nui Ba Den Mountain and saw the old radio post on top. It had been replaced by a religious pagoda. Stuart Simmons said he could see cable cars riding up and down the mountain. We continued to fly northward. The chopper began to circle a large open field surrounded by heavy woods. At one end we could see someone had popped smoke, marking our landing area. The pilot swung around, descending into the knee-high grass field and touched down. It felt weird not having my M-16 rifle in my hands as we prepared to climb off the helicopter.

We exited the chopper and walked toward the wood line. As we neared the trees, the chopper lifted off. We all shot looks of confusion to one another; watching the bird disappear over the tree line. Dave Whiteman said, "I really don't like the idea of approaching that wood line ahead. It would be great if Sarge or L.T. could still call in an artillery prep."

Doc answered, "Yeah, we sure had enough experiences being ambushed while walking into a strange wood line. This one looks much the same. What do you think is going on?"

"I hope someone has a cell phone for a taxi," Bob Tillis said. "It's a long walk home."

We looked around waiting to hear someone call out to us. The silence was eerie. Doc said, "Ah, come on.... Someone popped the smoke for us to land!"

"Gentlemen, Welcome." We could hear the squeal of a loud speaker. "I have arranged this outing today for my own enjoyment. Please walk toward the sound of the speaker as I explain today's events." We recognized General Toi's voice.

We obeyed and walked until we came upon a real bunker complex. Like a skip in time, we were back thirty years, with a feeling of having never left Vietnam. We could feel the anguish of fighting in complexes like this.

L.T. yelled out: "OK General. What the hell is going on? We're not amused or enjoying this. Let's call the chopper and head back."

"Silence!" the general yelled over the loud speaker.

"What the hell do you think he's up to?" Dave Whiteman asked. "We didn't come here to play games."

The speaker squealed again. "You have journeyed back to a place you encountered once before. Do you remember this place? It was you who stumbled onto this encampment during your time of duty here. Remember how you captured a young Vietnamese soldier? Perhaps he hid inside one of the bunkers or he was trapped below in the secret tunnel complex. Do you remember this place...? Do you remember him!"

Silence.

"Do you expect us to remember an incident like that... among so many encounters?" Sarge yelled back. His voice was strong and he spoke boldly, unafraid. "That was long ago, and now you want to play games ... what is it that you want?"

"What do I want? I want what every parent ... every brother or sister, aunt or uncle wants when they have lost a son to murderers. I want to avenge the end of my heritage ... a heritage you Company C men took from me. It was here my nephew was killed while held captive by you and your men. He was just a very young man. My family bloodline ceased with his death.

"Be careful what you say, men," Sergeant Browning cautioned. "I think our "gracious" host has flipped his lid."

"It was war, General," L.T. spoke out. "And how do you know it was us?"

"Listen to me men of Company C. All these years I have been researching the units that worked this area. You were an enemy I had fought many different times. Then finally, an opportunity came to visit your country ... you, at your reunion. Like magic, my wish came true. You were presented to me so conveniently. Now you will see what transpires when old soldiers meet again on the battle field."

Instinctively we had spread out. Some of the guys squatted or lay prone, expecting bullets to tear into our flesh at any moment. Once again, we looked to L.T. and Sarge to do the talking.

"General, you're dead wrong," L.T. said. "Yes, it's possible we did battle against each other. Surely, your nephew's death during a war should not be held as a lifelong death sentence. We sympathize with you on your nephew's death during a battle, but you must remember, it was a battle... two nations at war!"

We feared an uncertain fate. I wondered how the newspapers would carry it back home. I couldn't believe the madness of the General. Had he actually planned and schemed all of this many years ago? We were all trying to figure a method of quick escape.

"We are in one hell of a fix," Roser said. "We don't know our location, we have no communication, and most of us couldn't physically walk out of this jungle. No food, water or anything for our defense."

"Shit," Doc said. "I knew it back there in Nashville. I knew he was a phony."

"Guys, do any of you remember anything like the General described?" Sarge asked. He was extremely calm, considering the situation.

We could only shrug our shoulders and shake our heads. I didn't recall killing anyone around here. I didn't even recognize the place. An old familiar panic began to set in. There was a possibility that I might die in Vietnam after all. They say when you are near death, your life flashes before you. I don't know why, but suddenly I wanted to know the answer to a question that had been troubling me since I first joined the platoon. This might be my last chance to find out. "Roser, Roser," I called out. He was near me.

From his low crawl position behind a low berm, Roser answered. "What's that, Shorty?"

"Do you have a first name? ...never knew it."

"Jesus ... Why?"

"Just wanted to know ... maybe call you by your first name.

"Yes, I have a first name. ...just never told too many people."

"What is it?"

"Why the hell are you asking me at a time like this?

"What is it...? C'mon..."

"It's Bufford..."

"They called you Bufford?"

"Worse ... they called me Buffy."

"Buffy! And you carried a machine gun?"

"Stuff a sock in it, Shorty. You're the only guy I know that wants to know somebody's personal business even when he's laying on his deathbed."

"Did you kill the general's nephew... Buffy?"

I never knew why it was, but humor always seemed to sustain me during tough times and this was no exception. I laughed silently. *Buffy*!

"What the hell are you two chattering about," Sarge barked. "Do any of you know anything about what this madman is talking about?"

John Meddos said, "I think I may recall a similar incident... just maybe."

"Go ahead, anything could help," L.T, said.

"Remember the time Shorty went down a tunnel and caught that NVA trying to escape out another opening," John offered. "He shot him in the ass. Then I think our guys captured him."

"Yeah! That's right," Doc said. "Seems Standish and Shorty also got hurt some. I patched them up. I remember the Viet Cong unit counterattacked and used mortars. That's what killed the young VC."

"I do recall that," Sarge said. "They killed his nephew... not us. Does anyone remember anything else?"

"Roser's name is Buffy," I said.

"What? What the hell's that got to do with anything?" Sarge yelled.

"Nothing. I just thought you'd like to know," I yelled back.

"Shorty's flipped his lid," Roser said. "Maybe we ought to tell the general he did it and offer him up as a sacrificial lamb."

"I was just kidding, Roser," I said.

"Knock it off guys, come on... anything else?" L.T. said.

No one replied. "Okay then, let's see if I can get this screwball general to sit down and talk. We must convince him that this was all a mistake, an error in war. Neither side is responsible for his nephew's death. It is just one of those tragedies of war."

L.T. called out: "General ... General Toi! If you can hear me ... then hear this! We do remember the day of your nephew's death. We can also tell you his last moments ... his bravery. But most important, we can show you the person responsible."

Person responsible...? They're going to throw me to the wolves...!

L.T. continued his negotiations. "General Toi, if you continue this game of yours, you may never know whether your nephew died as a soldier, a coward, or a hero. The decision is yours." The awesome silence was becoming unbearable.

Like an apparition, the general appeared from the heavy brush. At his side were several well-armed soldiers. General Toi walked slowly towards us. His face was a blank stare, perhaps hiding his anger or his sorrow. "Tell me of my nephew. How was he murdered? Tell me quickly or you all will die!"

Two of our guys who had been standing, sank to the ground. The tension and anxiety weakened them until they were almost sick. We were all angry and scared. We knew our very lives depended on L.T. and his ability to show the general that his nephew's death was an accident of war—that he died an honorable soldier.

L.T. told General Toi about his nephew's capture as he tried to escape the tunnel. He explained how he had stayed to hide the tunnel complex and it secrets until his very last possible chance of escape. He told him about his wound and how he had been humanely treated. General Toi interrupted: "It was the short one you call a Tunnel Rat who is responsible?"

I almost crapped a cupcake. I knew my execution was seconds away as two of the soldiers pointed their AK-47s in my direction.

"No, listen please. Listen to what I have to say," L.T. said. "Yes, it was our man who slightly wounded your nephew.

Payback

But it was also these men who had our own physician attend to him. Your nephew was well and his wound was minor." L.T. was standing, face to face with the general. He seemed to be making some headway. We all stood to support him.

"What else," the general snapped. "How did he die?"

L.T. continued with Sarge standing right next to him. "Then our enemy—your men, General—made a counter attack to recapture this complex and secure the release of your nephew. But as merciless as war is, those same soldiers trying to free him used mortars as support for their attack. Your mortars killed your nephew and wounded my soldiers. You see, General Toi... your nephew was a brave soldier. If you must place a blame for his death, let it be charged to history. We all died a little from that war, and from that battle in particular. We are all soldiers here, not murderers. We need to forgive what we could not influence at that time."

General Toi looked long into L.T.'s eyes, then to each of us. "I have looked for revenge for a lifetime," he said. "I have searched the world for what has tormented me so long. When I found what I long looked for, my mind showed me the way to end my suffering. Revenge! It sounded so sweet."

"Is it, General?" L.T. asked.

"No.... I have found only brave men who also call my nephew a brave man. Now I know the true character of my enemy. I looked into your eyes in a time of certain death and you honored me. You honored my lifeline."

We could see the torment leaving his eyes. The general wiped them and ordered: "Go to the open field. The helicopter will arrive and fly you back. I can only say thank you and ask you to forgive me. I am a foolish old man." He saluted us, then he and his men walked away, disappearing into the jungle. We all cried a little walking back to the field. "I'll bet a million bucks the guys won't believe this at our next reunion!" Doc said.

I nodded. "Guys, speaking of not believing.... Do you know what Roser's first name is!"

EPILOGUE

*T*his is a story like any other. Some of it is true, but mostly it is fiction. As a Vietnam veteran, I always remember the bad times, the fun times, and even the dumb times. But what I remember most is how we American soldiers could always rely on each other, trust one another. I've never forgotten any one of them. This story is to honor their friendship and their memory.

The years passed quickly after my tour in Vietnam. I remember clearly the events, even after more than thirty years. I was proud to serve my country and to serve with all those great men. I am always willing to explain my tour in Vietnam, if anyone is interested enough to ask.

That year I served is permanently branded in my mind. I never felt special for being there until my first reunion. Yes, we do have real reunions, reunions that I wouldn't miss for the world. My only regret is there haven't been enough of them for every soldier who served in that tragic war.

After Vietnam, I returned to Wisconsin and became an auto body repairman. Later, my wife, Linda and I moved to Florida where I became a police officer. I felt like a soldier again.

God bless and continue to bless all those men I served with in Vietnam, and the police officers in Tampa, FL, with whom I now serve.

Shorty Menendez
Tunnel Rat at large.